BY JUSTINE CHAMPINE

Knife River

Needle Lake

Needle Lake

Needle Lake

A NOVEL

JUSTINE CHAMPINE

THE DIAL PRESS
NEW YORK

The Dial Press
An imprint of Random House
A division of Penguin Random House LLC
1745 Broadway
New York, NY 10019
randomhousebooks.com
penguinrandomhouse.com

Hardcover ISBN 9780593447239
Ebook ISBN 9780593447246

Printed in the United States of America on acid-free paper

1st Printing

FIRST EDITION

BOOK TEAM: Production editor: Dennis Ambrose • Managing editor: Rebecca Berlant • Production manager: Ali Wagner • Copy editor: Tom Cherwin • Proofreaders: Caryl Weintraub, Ruth Anne Phillips, and Michael Burke

Title-page art: Oleksii Nykonchuk/Adobe Stock

Book design by Ralph Fowler

The authorized representative in the EU for product safety and compliance is Penguin Random House Ireland, Morrison Chambers, 32 Nassau Street, Dublin D02 YH68, Ireland. https://eu-contact.penguin.ie

For autistic girls in every place and time

Needle Lake

1

My name is Ida. I was raised in Mineral, Washington, a logging town on the border of a vast national forest three hours north of Seattle. My mother owned a convenience store, which was situated on the ground floor of our home on the town's main street. It was a two-story building that had once housed a local paper, *The Mineral Star*. These words were painted in faded blue letters along the side of the building, five-point stars accentuating the swoops of the *S*. My mother and I lived in the rooms in the back, behind the store, and rented out the rooms on the top floor to the loggers. There was a single gas pump out front, and a coin laundry in the basement. I was responsible for emptying out the coins into a bucket every Sunday and counting them out on a table, rolling them into color-coded wrappers, and walking them to the bank. I was not to run to the bank. I was not supposed to run at all. I was born with a hole in my heart, large enough to sometimes cause me to faint, small enough to avoid operation in the opinion of the cardiologist at the hospital where I first entered the world. Twice a year I went to the cold, iodine-smelling office of our local, ancient Dr. Fields to be examined, an icy stethoscope pressed against my bare chest, his milky blue eyes magnified under thick glasses, gazing at the wall behind me as he listened. I was always smaller than other girls my age. Gaunt and bony where they'd all begun to grow. I was confined to the school library during gym class, never permitted to play dodgeball or horse or to climb the ropes.

I was entranced by the globe that sat in the corner of the library by the card catalog, far from the librarian who perched like a hawk on her elevated platform behind the checkout desk, date stamp in hand, scowling. I was in love with geography. I could place every country on a blank map, name its capital, identify its flag. I won a five-hundred-dollar municipal bond in the 1996 junior state geography bee. The runner-up, a boy from Tacoma, mislabeled the region of Sikkim as being a part of Bhutan and left me to answer the final question: How many islands make up the Philippines? Seven thousand, six hundred, and forty-one. When I couldn't fall asleep at night, which was often, I went through an alphabetical list of countries and their capitals in my mind. The process made me feel like my brain was being slowly submerged into a warm bath.

I loved salt and vinegar potato chips, honing pencils into fine points on the hand-cranked wall sharpeners at school, the smell of mothballs, the sound of crickets, the way orange goldfish looked inside round glass bowls, heart-shaped chocolate boxes for Valentine's Day with white lace trim and pillowy sateen covers, how a cat's eyes shined in the dark, green olives from a can. And, even though I wasn't supposed to, I secretly loved to swim. I loved to sneak out to the dock at Needle Lake early summer mornings before anyone else was around. I loved the moment my body first sliced through the water's surface, the way the noise of the world muffled into a soft quiet and everything went slow and blue. I could hold my breath for ninety-six seconds, on average, though I once stayed under for one hundred and one. Sometimes I saw snapping turtles huddled on mossy rocks, asleep. I found things on the bottom. Glasses, an unopened bottle of gin, a metal toy train. A gold wedding band, glistening in the silt.

And once, after Elna came to stay, I watched a man drown there on Christmas Eve, his body trapped beneath the ice.

2

My cousin Elna arrived mid-December the year I was fourteen. I didn't even know she'd been invited to stay. I'd only seen her a single time before, when I was in first grade, at our grandfather's funeral in Coeur d'Alene, Idaho. Autumn of 1990. The memory was a blur to me: the chalky, sweet smell of white flowers, six tall men in dark coats on either side of a lacquered casket, and, faintly, Elna, staring at me from the other side of the grave site as the dirt was piled on.

I was sitting behind the cash register looking at one of my maps when the bells on the front door rattled. A tall, slim, red-headed girl in a mint green winter coat was standing there, looking around. She had two bags with her, both also green, and was wearing a pair of silver winter boots. She was very pretty. From twenty feet away, I could see that. I blinked at her, baffled, and before I could open my mouth to say anything my mother came swooping in from the back room in her coveralls, securing the red-haired girl in a firm, two-handed grip on the shoulders. They spoke some muffled words to each other, too faint for me to hear at the other end of the store, and then walked past all the shelves over to where I was seated at the counter. The girl shook some snow out of her long hair, fluffing up her bangs with her fingers. I noticed that her nails were painted a bright, pearlescent pink, filed into slender ovals. She wore several rhinestone rings, a shiny gold charm bracelet, and a pair of star-shaped earrings with little purple crystals in them.

"Ida," my mother said. "You remember your cousin." It took me a moment to understand who, exactly, that was. Apart from the hair, she looked nothing like the child I distantly remembered.

"Hello," I said.

My mother went on, "She's going to stay with us for a little while. Maybe through January."

Elna gave a coy half-smile to neither of us in particular and placed both her bags on the ground. She slipped out of her wet snow boots and began to wander around the store, stocking-footed. She inspected the place slowly, prowling between the shelves like a panther dropped in a new enclosure, skittish and aloof at the same time. She tapped her nails on the glass refrigerator case, then turned to us and said in a wispy voice, "I've had a very long bus ride," before brushing aside the curtain that divided the store from our living area and slipping out of view. My mother paused uncertainly mid-step with her hands outstretched toward Elna's suitcases. I almost never saw her like that. She was always in motion: hauling bulk shipments of beer and canned beans in from the curb, chasing a bat or a raccoon out of the store with a broomstick, lugging twenty-pound jugs of detergent down to fill the pay dispenser in the basement laundry. But now she was very still. It made me uneasy.

I looked at Elna's empty shoes. "She's here alone?" I asked.

My mother cleared her throat. "Your aunt Candace isn't coming," she said.

"Why not?"

"She isn't well right now."

"What do you mean?"

"She's having a lot of problems." My mother and I did not discuss her sister often. Sometimes, I overheard the two of them on the phone. I could always tell when it was Candace on the line. The conversations took on a hushed, tense tone. It didn't sound angry to me, not like the tension of an argument, but more worried, with a fraught closeness that was hard for me to understand though unmistakable in the sound of my mother's voice.

I'd only met my aunt twice—first at the same funeral in Idaho where I met Elna, and then another time when she visited on my tenth birthday, without her daughter, just for the day. She brought me a brilliant pink spiral seashell, with a softly worn fifty-dollar bill wedged inside. My mother deposited this money at the bank. Candace drove back that night to where she was staying in Seattle with an ex-boyfriend, after she and my mother took a long cigarette walk together. I remember seeing them folded into a hug from my bedroom window. Candace had a bag at her feet with some sundries from our shop. Gifts, I understood. Her car was banged up around the sides and had many glittery stickers on the back, two plastic rosaries dangling from the rearview mirror, and a steering wheel cover made of fake purple fur. I knew she lived in San Francisco. I knew she had appeared in a handful of commercials, and in three episodes of a TV drama. She was two years younger than my mother. I got the sense she'd always had a lot of problems.

I could hear Elna in the back, her feet shuffling in the hall, the sound of a glass being set on a counter, the bathroom faucet going on and off. "No one told me she was coming," I huffed.

"No one needs to tell you anything," my mother replied. "Least of all me."

"Where's she going to sleep?" I asked. "Upstairs is full."

"She's not staying upstairs with the tenants, even if there was space. She'll stay in the spare room next to yours."

"It's full of boxes."

"I'll move them."

"There isn't even a bed in there."

"We have an extra cot."

"How long have you known she was coming?"

"I wasn't completely sure until she arrived, honestly. I've told you how your aunt can be." My mother picked up Elna's bags and carried them to the threshold of our rooms, then turned around and looked at me. "You don't mind her being here for a little bit?" she asked, her voice now hesitant and very quiet.

I could tell she wanted reassurance more than anything else, but I answered honestly. "How can I know if I'll mind or not if she's only been here for ten minutes?"

"I mean do you think you *will* mind?"

I craned my neck around and saw Elna through a space in the curtain, flitting between the bathroom and the spare room, which she'd clearly already figured out was meant for her to stay in. Her winter coat had come off. She was wearing a purple miniskirt and a matching sweater with a glittery butterfly on the chest. I watched as she paused on her way into the bedroom, toiletry case in hand, stopping to look at a picture in the hallway. It was a photograph I'd taken last summer, of my mother and Jen, her girlfriend, in the yard behind the store. They'd just rebuilt the back porch together. There was white paint smeared on their faces. Elna reached up and straightened the frame, setting it even on the nail.

"I don't expect to mind," I finally said.

The store was open for another three hours. I watched the register while my mother helped get Elna settled in. One of the boarders, Charlie, came down to buy a box of cereal and some milk. He paid with exact change, like he always did, and retreated upstairs. His steps came as a slow, echoing creak as he made his way back to the third floor. An older girl I recognized from my school came in to buy a large bag of barbecue chips. I could tell she didn't know who I was. Two other girls were idling in a car parked out front, waiting for her, playing music. After that, no one else came in. I unfolded the map I'd been looking at earlier and spread it across the counter. It was a close-up depiction of the Pacific Islands I'd recently gotten from a mail-order catalog. The ocean was colored in shades of blue, the variations indicating the way the depth leveled off near shore. It showed the highest point of elevation on each island, the trenches and ridges that sat between, rising up from the sea floor. I ran my finger across the Tropic of Capricorn. I recited the names of the atolls under my breath.

When my mother emerged from the basement with the cot, I stood to help her and was promptly shooed away. "What would Dr. Fields say?" she muttered, wrangling the metal frame with bare hands.

What he would've said was, *Limit exertion*. No horses, no bicycles, no gymnastics, no tree climbing, no leaping from barn windows into stacks of hay, no stickball, no tetherball, no relay races. Better not to risk the annual presidential fitness test. Best to sit out of gym period altogether. He'd given permission for me to learn how to swim years earlier, deeming it a safety precaution in our area with its many dozens of rivers and lakes, but lectured for a long five minutes about restraint. "Absolutely no cannonballs," he said. I could hear the low, droning croak of his voice coming round and round like a loop in my brain for weeks after. "No flinging yourself around like a fish. No underwater tea parties. No racing anybody to the bottom to collect coins, or what have you." I heard his voice loudest the first time I stood on the edge of the dock at Needle Lake, alone, in the early morning, my whereabouts unbeknownst to anyone but me, and threw myself from a running leap down below the surface. Once I was underwater, I couldn't hear him anymore.

3

That night, I heard rustling in the shop and got out of bed to look. Sometimes a possum or something found its way in and needed to be chased out. In winter, especially, animals snuck inside. But when I pushed the divider curtain aside, I saw Elna crouched in front of the refrigerator case, a sandwich in one hand and a strawberry Crush in the other. At her feet was a torn-open package of vanilla wafers. She looked like an apparition out there in the dark room: makeup scrubbed off and her pale skin shimmering with a film of night cream, illuminated by a backlit glow, lips stained red from the soda. She was wearing an oversized T-shirt, pale green like her coat and bags, a lavender flower with a smiley face center emblazoned on the chest. Her bare legs were long and spindly. Her eyelashes were translucent. I got the sense that she saw me standing there, but she didn't look up. She took a large bite from the sandwich and a whole slice of tomato came slipping out, which she grabbed with her teeth and tossed back into her mouth efficiently, almost elegantly, like a kingfisher hunting at dusk.

I went over and sat on the floor near her. I felt suddenly aware of how I looked, how Elna might see me, and smoothed down my hair in the back. I was wearing mismatched flannel pajamas, long-sleeved top and bottom. My eyes were crusted over. I noticed that her toenails were painted the same pearlescent pink as her fingers. I curled my toes under and tugged the hem of my pants down to cover my feet.

Still not looking at me, she said, "I'm starving. I hope you don't mind. All I had on the bus was a bag of peanuts and a chocolate bar." I told her I didn't mind.

She finished the sandwich, the soda, and all the cookies, then sat back against the cold-case and set her gaze on me. I looked at the floor, then at my hands, then at the space between her eyes above the bridge of her nose. It was a trick I'd come up with when direct eye contact felt too prickly. It worked better on adults. They didn't seem to notice. But kids usually did.

Elna scrunched her face up at me and after a moment of consideration asked, "You're fourteen now?"

"Yes."

"I'm almost seventeen." I let out a grunt of acknowledgment. "You still have that heart thing?" she asked.

I nodded, then said, "It's not a big deal."

"No?"

"I haven't fainted in a while."

"Does it hurt? When you're just walking around, I mean." It

wasn't a simple question. It didn't hurt like a hornet's sting, or a finger slammed in a door, but sometimes the hole would cause my heart to skip a group of beats in a row. Those moments of stillness in my chest were scary and weirdly peaceful at the same time. The feeling of my body's most vital, constant rhythm brought to a sudden halt, and the sensation of floating that went along with it. A strange weightlessness, like being only half alive. It wasn't usually painful so much as it was the absence of a feeling altogether.

"No," I finally replied. "It doesn't hurt."

"Do you miss a lot of school for it?"

"Sometimes. Mostly just gym, though."

"Why weren't you there today? You were here in the store when I showed up at like eleven in the morning."

"It's the first week of winter break," I said. "I don't have to go back until after the New Year."

"Oh, right." She nodded slowly before adding, "Your mother has you taking shifts?"

"A few times a week," I explained. "Mostly in the mornings. Sometimes when she's making dinner."

"She pay you?"

"No," I told her.

Elna rolled her eyes, then said, "I stopped going to school."

"You dropped out?"

"In October. But I didn't technically drop out, I took a leave. I had to forge my mother's signature. I'm not going back, though."

"Your mother doesn't care?"

She paused, blinking at me in disbelief before saying, "She doesn't *know.*"

We sat quietly for a minute. The only sound was the hum of the soda case. Then I blurted out, "Why *are* you here?"

A kind of wry smile passed over her lips and then vanished. "No one told you?"

"No."

"Oh," she said. She seemed to be thinking to herself, lips parted, the glint of a tooth shining between them. "My mom got another DUI and got a choice between detox or thirty days in jail. I told her I could just stay in the apartment alone, but she suddenly got all responsible and said no. Probably she's just worried someone will realize there's an unattended minor and she'll get in worse trouble."

"So, she chose the detox."

"Yeah," Elna said. "Obviously."

"Where is she now?"

"Some place in San Jose. I think she's been to this one before. She's gone to like, four of these now."

"Oh."

"She doesn't even drink. I mean, she does, but it's fine. She's just a huge pillhead." My cousin held her hands up to her face and pulled the skin of her temples back slightly, eyes closed, grimacing. Her breathing had quickened and the corners of her lips were tight, downturned.

"What kind of pills does she take?" I asked.

"What kind of pills doesn't she take?" I looked at Elna, unsure of how to respond. "I don't have a clue anymore," Elna went on. "I don't use any of that shit. I've seen her fall asleep standing up. Like, literally standing up holding a plate of food. It broke all over the floor in a million little pieces and she barely even blinked. She just stood there with her eyes half closed while I swept it into the dustpan."

My cousin shook her head quickly, like she was shaking the memory out of it. Then, she cast her eyes into a downward glance and asked, "Are you cool with me being here?"

"Yes," I told her, "of course," though really, I didn't exactly know how I felt about it. One moment she was a vague recollection I'd had, the next she was five foot nine with pierced ears and a manicure, breathing the same air as me. The pores on her nose were incredibly small. Her ears were small, too, pressed flat against her head. I studied the way her hairline faded into her forehead in a precise, symmetrical half-circle.

"Good," she replied, then added, "let's see your room." She got up quickly, leaving her food wrappings on the floor and brushing crumbs off her shirt as she walked. Even like this, she was poised. Somehow glamorous in her sleep T-shirt. Different than anyone I'd seen in real life. We got monthly shipments of magazines to the store and one of my jobs was organizing them on the rack by the door. In the past couple years, I'd grown increasingly fascinated with the glossy, candy-colored ones meant for girls slightly older than me. I flipped past the celebrities to find all the fashion spreads. Not because I wanted the things pictured in them, but because I was enamored of the images, these distillations of teenhood, perfectly arranged. Three girls in a futuristic, orange room, all sitting on a white couch, wearing matching white satin pajamas, eating popcorn out of a white bowl, giggling into one white telephone. The next page, a platform-sandaled girl on an inflatable chair holding a Magic 8 Ball up to the lens, nails and eyelids painted silver, her abundance of blond hair secured with rows of sparkly butterfly clips. They were all icy smiles and good posture. The right combination of charm and aloofness. Elna seemed to have the same thing I saw in these pictures. It wasn't just what she wore, it was the way she spoke, the presence of her silence, how she seemed to glide rather than walk. She was self-possessed, confident, a little standoffish in a way that made me want to be around her even more.

My old teacher Ms. Sellers, who I considered my friend, had once noticed me studying one of these magazines in the library at school. She sat down at the table and gently said, "It's all professional lighting. And some digital manipulation." I looked at her and understood she must have thought these images made me insecure, worried about how I looked or what I didn't have in my closet. This was not the case. I didn't think about myself at all when I studied them. I told her I knew, and she sat there for another minute, a limp smile on her face and her forehead bunched together before giving me a light pat on the shoulder and walking out into the hall. I kept my eyes on the magazine as she left. It was like there was this invisible fence that ran down the center of girlhood, dividing those who had *it,* the thing from the pictures, the thing Elna seemed to have, and those who didn't and either longed for it or rejected it knowingly. I didn't feel like I was on one side or the other. It felt more like I was standing in a field away from the fence altogether, watching everything carefully.

Elna flicked the light on in my room before I could get to it. She took a step in and spun around slowly. There were maps everywhere. The walls, my desk, rolled up on the bookshelf, taped to the ceiling. Seeing all my things through her eyes gave me a lurch in the stomach. I felt like I needed to do something, explain myself, but I just stood off to the side, arms crossed, while she walked around slowly. She spun my globe around a couple times and brought her face close to the big world map, squinting at the fine print over the Bering Strait. Then she took the desk chair, twirled it around, and sat backward on it, her elbows perched on the top.

"You like maps, I guess," she said.

"Yeah," I replied.

"Why?"

I shrugged. I didn't really know *why* I liked maps so much. Why maps and not horses or scrapbooking or watercolors. They'd drawn me in since I first saw the world on a globe in the library at school. Looking at them, it was easy to fall into something like a trance, like I was drifting on a stream, moving steadily, the rush of cold water quickening my breath, eyes fixed on the horizon. It was like stepping into an entirely different dimension. It lit my brain up. I could study them for hours and feel still that there was more to understand about them, new subtleties to notice. I would've explained it to Elna, but the feeling broke down and fell back into me before it could reach my lips. My mother sometimes said I was like a kettle missing its spout. *I can't get you out of yourself,* she would complain.

I was anxious that Elna would press the question, but she didn't. She just nodded, then said, "Flags, too," flicking her chin at a blue ceramic vase that held a collection of miniature flags on spindles, all of which I'd gotten by writing to different embassies and cultural centers, stating my age and location along with the request. So far I had Greenland, Nepal, the Seychelles, Wales, Togo, Bahrain, India, Canada, Chile, Latvia, Palau, Micronesia, and New Zealand. I was still waiting to hear back from Sweden.

"Flags, too," I repeated.

Elna then rose from the chair and went straight to my closet, where she began sifting through the hangers, pausing to examine some things and pushing others aside. She crouched down and peered at my shoes. She crawled up to the long mirror which hung on the inside of the closet door and flipped her hair around a couple times, pinching at the bangs, making tiny adjustments to the part. No one but myself or my mother had been in my bedroom since last summer when I turned thirteen. I felt absolutely frozen in place. She pulled out a checkerboard-patterned windbreaker and held it up, angling toward her reflection.

"This is actually kind of cool," she said. "Where did you get it?"

"Someone left it here."

"What, like, in the store?"

"No," I told her. "One of the boarders. Sometimes they just leave stuff when they move out."

"And you get to keep it?"

"We put it in boxes and if they don't come back for it within a month then, yeah. Or we throw it out, or sell it if it's worth anything."

"What kind of stuff do they leave?"

"Usually a bunch of junk." I thought of a tenant who'd moved out last fall and left garbage strewn everywhere. Not just discarded belongings, but the kind of trash you'd find in a kitchen bin. Oily paper plates and chicken bones all over the floor. Broken bottles with syrupy, fermenting liquid in the bottom. Used tissues piled high on the windowsill. My mother and I stood there in the doorway, gloves on, grimacing at the mess. Amongst it all, a snow globe with a little mountain inside. *Mt. Rainier, 14,411 ft*, in block letters on the base. I would've kept it, but it was cracked and leaking. We used brooms to push all the debris into a yard bag. "But sometimes not," I added. "Sometimes they leave books or clothes that are pretty good." I nodded toward the jacket. Elna put it on and zipped it halfway up. It looked right on her. I got the sense that anything would.

"What will you do when you go back to San Francisco?" I asked.

"What do you mean?" By now Elna was sitting on my bed with her legs up against the wall, spinning her feet around in lazy circles.

"Since you aren't going back to school."

"Oh," she said. "Well, I have some ideas. Firstly, I don't want to stay there for too long. I want to move to LA." At this she rolled over and lay on her stomach, chin propped up on one wrist. "My friend moved there after leaving school and makes a lot of money showing up to kids' parties dressed as characters. She leaves flyers on the windshields of cars in the Disneyland overflow parking lots. So, I figure I'll do that with her for a while."

"I guess you'd be Ariel," I said. "Because of your hair."

"Right," she smirked. "And what about you?" I blinked. A small smile cracked the corner of her lip. "Before you know it, you'll graduate high school. Are you going to stay here ringing up pork rinds?"

"Probably not."

"Then, what?"

I hadn't really thought much about my future beyond the next year or so. Only in a wide, dreamy sort of way. I knew there was a type of cartographer whose job was to map the ocean floor. I didn't know much about how it worked, other than it involved echoes bouncing from the ship down all the way through the depths of the sea and back again. Whole portraits of the world were made this way. Sometimes I could picture a distant version of myself floating along the deep water, shining instruments all around me, collecting the echoes.

I cleared my throat and replied, "I suppose I'll have to see what the results of my career aptitude test say." She looked at me like I was insane, laughed a little bit, then rolled off the bed and stood, stretching her arms and yawning. I had actually meant to be funny. Our school made everyone take a test like that in their senior year. I'd seen copies of it coming off the library Xerox. There were questions like, *If you were a plant, would you thrive in the shade or the sun?*

"All right," Elna said. "I need to get some sleep. I'll see you later." She sauntered into the hallway, still wearing the checkerboard jacket from my closet, and shut the door behind her.

4

The next day, when my mother took over for me at the register around noon, I brought Elna out for a walk around Mineral. She wanted to know where everything was, who everyone was, why all the activity was confined to such a small area.

"Less than two thousand people live here," I told her. "More this time of year. Now is actually the busy season."

"Winter?"

"It's when most of the logging is done. So, there's a lot of seasonal workers." Just up the road, an enormous flatbed truck, laden with lumber, began its slow turn toward the highway. "When there's snowpack," I said, "it's easier to take trees down without damaging the soil layer." She nodded, surveying the street from underneath her sunglasses. They were white plastic, oversized, with elongated oval lenses that blacked out her eyes completely. I thought they made her look famous.

We walked first down the smaller street behind our shop, which led to my school, a car dealership, Dr. Fields' office, a small tattoo parlor, and an ice-cream shop. When we passed the doctor's office, I found myself turning my head slightly down and away from the door, picking up my steps just a little. I didn't want to talk about my heart again. I almost wished Elna didn't know about it at all.

Three more lumber trucks turned on the road ahead, the groan of their tire chains echoing out in rusty, stilted heaves. I clenched my teeth. The noise went on as the trucks struggled to make the corner. We waited at the crossing light while another one drove past, the smell of sap and loam thick in the air. I could hear the individual logs scraping up against one another. In my mind, quickly, I went diving underwater, which was what I imagined for myself whenever something became unbearable. I came up with it the first time I had to eat lunch in the school cafeteria, and the sounds of a hundred chewing mouths and different voices competing to be heard felt like two dental drills bearing straight into my eardrums. There was the heavy clack of the old lady lunch monitor's black, pointed shoes as she stalked the perimeter of the tables. A big metal serving spoon thwacking against the edge of a hot dish. Fluorescent lights buzzing overhead. And then it was like a door in my brain swung open into a place where I could pop my head in and breathe: a deep lake full of glowing, blue water, the air still and cold, utterly silent. After that, I went there all the time.

"Are you all right?" Elna asked.

"Fine," I told her. I forced my face into its relaxed position. The truck had passed by, and we crossed the street together. I could tell she was looking at me but I kept staring ahead. Once we got to the main part of town, I pointed out the movie theater, the grocery store, the hair salon, the shoe store. She stopped in front of the shoe store's window and looked at her reflection, pushing her sunglasses up on top of her hair. There was a display of patent leather Mary Janes arranged on top of wrapped boxes with big, shiny bows. Green, red, gold paper. The littlest pair could've fit in my palm. All the shoes I'd ever owned in my life had come from this store. Farther down the street, outside the electronics dealer, Elna asked me if I liked living in Mineral.

"It's fine," I told her. "I don't have anywhere else to compare it to."

"What do people do for fun?"

"They go fishing, I think."

"Fishing?"

"Well, I see a lot of people with like, fishing equipment on the weekends."

"Quaint."

Just then, a carload of young guys slowed down as they passed us. The driver stared at Elna, then the rest of them craned their necks to look at her, too. One of them tipped his baseball hat at her. She rolled her eyes and sighed. The car moved along, leaving our view.

"Do you have a boyfriend?" I asked.

"No," she said. "I did over the summer, but I dumped him."

"Why?"

"He grew a beard. It really grossed me out."

"I don't have a boyfriend, either," I told her.

"I know," she said.

We walked in silence for a few minutes. Gray clouds rolled in over the mountains on the horizon. From the sidewalk, I could see Mount Baker rising up from the mist. Stark and jagged and imposing, draped in snow. Below it, tiers of evergreen and alpine lakes. Somewhere in there, far from the mountain, was the place I secretly went to swim in the summer. If I walked all the way up this block, turned onto the old logging road, and took a short hike, I'd be there.

"Where can I get some hair spray?" Elna asked. "I forgot to bring any."

We went into the variety store, a massive and drafty place that smelled strongly of potting soil year-round. They sold not just gardening supplies and animal feed, but all manner of novelty candy, cosmetics, and magic tricks. There was a whole wall of fossils and minerals for sale, a table with ladies' stockings, men's socks, children's underwear, artificial flowers in barrels, plastic dolls in plastic bags hanging on a tall pegboard, lava lamps, snow shovels, string lights, corded telephones in a rainbow of colors. There were some people inside doing their pre-Christmas shopping. An old lady pushed a rickety cart full of ornaments. Down the way, there was a group of teenagers standing around the CD rack.

"Do you know them?" Elna asked. "They look about your age."

"They go to my school. They're a year ahead of me."

"What are their names?"

"I have no idea," I said. I'd never actually met them, but even if I had I wouldn't have had anything to tell her. People didn't stick with me the way other things did. Their names came into my ears and fell straight out. The group looked at Elna, studying her with interest. She gave them a once-over and then kept walking up the aisle with me. I glanced back at them and found that they were still watching her, though clearly trying to appear as though they weren't.

I hung back as Elna dug through a bin full of hair accessories. I was anxious that someone, either the group of high schoolers or a cashier who may've recognized me or anyone on the street, might approach me wanting to find out who was this new girl I was walking around with. I imagined how the conversation would go. I'd tell them this was my cousin, that she was visiting from California, that she'd be in Mineral for maybe a month or so. They would want to chat, and there would have to be smiling. Just the idea of it made a nervous heat rise up my neck. I was so used to moving within the little world of my town more or less unnoticed. People didn't talk to me much. I didn't have the kind of mother who pushed me to mingle with other kids my age. Now, the simple fact of Elna's presence caused eyes to follow. She held three scrunchies together, comparing the colors, then turned and flashed me a quick smile. Her teeth were nice. No spaces or funny angles between them. I wanted to hang out with her, I really did. I just didn't want to be noticed.

We moved through the aisles side by side, browsing all the

shiny Christmas things. A crackly speaker played pop renditions of old-fashioned carols overhead. When we approached the corner where all the fishing lures were stocked, Elna tapped her fingers along the back of my arm and whispered, "What about her? Does she go to your school?"

I squinted ahead at a girl with a long, dark braid looking through the packaged bait. I studied her profile, trying to get a clear view of her face. I wasn't sure if I'd ever seen her or not. Probably, yes. Most of the kids in Mineral were all penned in the same place every weekday: two big brick buildings in a cleared-out field, connected by a path, one for kindergarten through sixth, the other through twelfth. The rest were homeschooled. My mother occasionally commented that this might've been the better option for me, but who would do the teaching? She barely had time to keep her hair washed, she liked to say. I told her I was capable of doing it myself and even though she always said *Absolutely not,* I got the sense she didn't totally disagree.

The girl turned in to the next aisle without facing us. I shrugged and shook my head. "Who are your friends, then?" Elna asked.

"I don't really hang out with anyone, anymore," I admitted.

"Why not?" At this I just stared at her, blankly. No one had ever asked me to explain it before. Elna spun around a wire carousel of holographic stickers, not taking her eyes off it as she spoke to me. It was like she was interested in my answers, but didn't really care that much. Interested the way you might be in overhearing a minor argument in the next booth at a diner if your food was running late. It made the questions easier for me to take. It made me like her more.

"Just don't," I said.

"But you used to?" she asked.

"Yeah, I used to hang out with two girls from my year but one of them moved to Boise and the other one, Julie, won't speak to me now."

"You had a fight?"

"Well, no. I don't think so. She just stopped talking to me."

"Just like that?" Elna said, pinching a piece of lint off my shoulder and blowing it from her finger.

"Kind of. I mean, I don't know what happened. We have math together this year and she doesn't even look at me." Before Elna came in to flip through my closet the other night, Julie was actually the last person to have hung out in my room. She used to come over a lot. Her parents were in the military and she'd lived in a lot of different places. I was always asking her to point them out on one of my maps. I placed small, golden star stickers over all the locations. Seven, in total. Three continents.

"She sounds like a real bitch, then," Elna scoffed, taking me by the hand and walking me over to the makeup counter. It was unattended by any employee, despite having a little chair and its own register behind the chrome glass. All my life, I'd never seen anyone working back there. There were displays of eye shadows and blushes laid out on cheap, gold-brushed plastic tiers. The samples were all worn down, the powder cakes dried out and cracking around the corners. It looked like the owner had purchased a whole cosmetics counter from a failed department store, plopped it in the back of this five-and-dime, and then forgotten about it.

Elna dragged her finger through a pan of gray eye shadow, then tapped it on my eyelids and blended it out carefully. She took a step back, looked me over, then grabbed a dark eye pencil. She pulled a lighter from her pocket and held the liner tip over the flame, rotating it a couple times. I could see the wax softening in the heat. Then, quickly, she flicked the pencil around the corners of my eyelids, smudging it into the roots of my lashes with her knuckle. Normally, I wasn't crazy about getting my face touched. The last time our school nurse administered our annual sight test, I stood up from the chair abruptly, knocking over a potted fern, when she came at me with the eye cover. The whole line of kids behind me erupted into snickers. In the end, I held the cover myself, whispering the letters on the wall poster while the nurse frowned at me. But now, here in the back of the store, I tolerated Elna's prodding and dabbing, trying hard to keep still the whole time. She spun me around toward the mirror. There were our two faces reflected back: hers still bright and rosy from the cold, mine suddenly sharper, more feminine than plainly girlish.

"What do you think?" she asked.

"It's nice," I said. I loved it.

"You should do this all the time. It looks good."

"I really don't know how," I told her. "I've never tried."

"I'll teach you," she said.

I didn't realize Elna was stealing until after we left. Halfway up the main street we turned into a little alcove between buildings to zip our coats up against the gathering wind, and she excitedly produced not just the hair spray I knew she wanted but handfuls of other small items from various pockets in her coat. I was floored. Plastic hair barrettes, a green velvet scrunchie, a bottle of lavender nail polish, a miniature bar of heart-shaped soap, sour candies in a metallic wrapper, cherry lip gloss, purple eyeliner, a mood ring. She pressed the ring into my palm and grinned. She was glowing. A pulsing, wild energy rose off her like steam. The ring changed color in my hand, black to orange to blue. Elna untwisted the lip gloss wand and glided the applicator across her lips. I could smell the artificial fruit additive, and something sweet and heavy hanging in the air.

I couldn't quite keep her pace as we went up the hill, so I hung back and watched the sweeping profile of her hair in the wind, the mood ring burning a hole in my grip.

5

The next morning, Elna emerged from the spare room with her hair pulled up in a fluffy, high ponytail. As she approached the register, I noticed it was held in place with the green velvet scrunchie she'd nicked from the variety store. I didn't want her to notice that I wasn't wearing the mood ring, so I curled my fingers into fists and held them beneath the counter. The ring was in a little box in my bedside drawer. I wasn't sure what to do with it. I woke up a couple times in the night and thought about it, even reaching into the drawer to touch it, worried and excited and a little nauseated all at the same time.

She didn't look at my hands at all. Instead, she pointed out the window to the covered porch attached to the shop and asked, "Are those all loggers?" There were men standing around in a disjointed group, smoking and drinking coffee. One of them was eating a packaged honey bun I'd sold to him twenty minutes earlier. I nodded.

"Do any of them board here?"

"About half of them."

"What're they doing out there?"

"They're waiting for the trucks to come by and pick them up to go out into the forest."

She stood with her hand on her hip, studying the men. While she watched them, I looked at her. There was mascara on her top and bottom lashes. She had a different pair of earrings on today: little rhinestone horseshoes. I could see that there were thoughts forming in her head, but I couldn't tell what they might be. I twisted my fingers around under the counter.

Finally, she said, "Back in a minute," and made her way to the front door. I saw her swivel through the doorway and reappear a moment later on the other side, smiling and tall, ponytail swinging. Every single one of the men stopped mid-motion and parted to let her through, their gaze leveled at her like feral dogs in a field. She made her way to the center of the porch and put her hand out for a cigarette, which she was promptly given. A different man lit it for her, and she stood there smoking with these strangers, grown adults, men, without any hint of awkwardness or apprehension. She held the cigarette delicately with the tips of her fingers, wrist arched. I could see that her mouth was moving the whole time, chatting and grinning. Her face was animated. Expressions passed easily over her eyes and mouth. None of it seemed forced. And each expression she made seemed to last exactly the right amount of time, coming and going as the conversation between them all went on. She pivoted from man to man, leaning her head in to listen as they chatted with her, laughing a little and nodding with what looked like just the right level of interest.

I first started practicing faces in front of the mirror when I was eight after school picture day. We all had to line up in the main hallway before a photographer, who took three shots of us each before beckoning the next student to come sit down on the wooden box. There was a blue sateen backdrop and a bright bucket light on a metal stand. When it was my turn, I sat on the box and waited for the click of the camera. The photographer told me to smile. I thought I already was. I tried to smile more, thinking that I probably needed to make more of my teeth visible. He frowned and told me to give him a *nice* smile. His voice had grown taut. Laughter began to erupt from the line. Even my friend, the one who would move away in a few years, was laughing. By then I was anxious, and itchy from the heat of the light beaming at my face. He got his three clicks in and I took the photo redemption slip from the hall attendant, who also frowned at me, and after school I went directly home to my room, where I sat at my desk, studying my reflection. I smiled again and again and again. My face grew sore.

I went out into the store and discreetly took a few magazines back to my room, studying the smiles of famous women and trying to copy the way their mouths spread across their faces. As I looked at the pictures, it became clear that there were all different ways. Hints of smiles that stayed mostly at the corners of the lips, big wet ones with many dazzling teeth, sly ones that appeared to hold something back. Some of them were even smiling with tears coming down their faces. It all made me a little dizzy. By now, this had become something I just did out of habit, like brushing my teeth or taking my vitamin. It was almost involuntary. Without even thinking about it I'd find myself practicing a few quick faces and hand gestures before leaving the bubble of my room every day. Somehow, I knew this was not something Elna had ever done.

When she came back in from the porch, I could feel the cold air coming off her. "I'm going to make some money sewing for the loggers," she announced.

"Sewing?"

"And laundry."

"What do you know about sewing?" I asked.

"A lot," she replied. "Anyway, their clothes get all ripped up out there; they need tons of repairs." I listened as she explained how they'd agreed to drop their dirty, torn things off with her after their shift, and she'd return them clean and free of holes.

"Did you come up with this idea just now?" I asked. I was a little awed by the whole thing. Just minutes earlier she'd been standing here knowing next to nothing about the men outside, and now she'd gotten a cigarette and the promise of money from them. She seemed to know all their names, too. She pointed out the window as the trucks approached and rattled them off, seemingly for her own retention, one by one, as they loaded into the cabs.

"And Charlie's from Coeur d'Alene," Elna said as the last truck drove off.

She gave me a little wink and a pinch on the cheek. I thought of her standing on the other side of my grandfather's grave in her long navy dress and shiny shoes. The Elna in the room with me now seemed like a different person, from a different life altogether, like a lingering dream I'd had.

"What do you think about three dollars for each load of laundry?" she asked.

"They pay a dollar in coins now just for the wash. It's another fifty cents to use the dryer. I think they'd pay you double to not have to do it themselves."

"Then maybe two fifty per mend," she said, brow furrowed. She did some counting on her fingers and nodded to herself.

We sat quietly for a few minutes. "It doesn't get very busy in here, does it," Elna finally said, picking at her cuticles.

"Not really."

"Don't you get bored sitting here all day?"

I reached under the counter into one of the compartments and pulled out my box of geography flash cards. "I usually go through these. I've been studying them for the next bee in September." Elna took the box and examined it, pulling out the first card from the deck and turning it around in her hand. On one side, the flag of Palau. On the other, a list of facts about Palau. "I really love that one," I blurted out. "I love all the flags with circles in their design."

"Who doesn't," she muttered.

"You do, too?" I asked.

"What? No. I've never even heard of Palau." She shook her head and read the back of the card. "All right." She sat up straight. "How many miles of coastline does this country have?"

"Nine hundred and forty-four."

"God," she said. "You are seriously so weird." I stared at her. She shuffled the cards around, pausing at Albania and passing it to the back of the deck. "One of my mom's boyfriends was from there," she said. "He owned a car wash."

"They also have a good flag."

"Mexico." She held the card up for a second. "I went there once." Elna tucked everything back in the box and placed it firmly on my lap. "You're actually pretty cute with these cards." Her tone was a little syrupy. It reminded me of the way someone would talk to a dog. She blinked her big green eyes at me and then added, in a more regular kind of voice, "I guess I don't have much to do until the guys drop their clothes off later."

"You could help me unpack this box of air fresheners." I gestured to the container on the floor behind us. This was one of the things I was allowed to open and put out on display, because they were so light there was no way I could strain my heart. I liked whenever a shipment arrived. Not just because it meant I got to do something in the store besides sitting at the till, but because I got to arrange each piece in rows by color on a little peg wall by the exit. They were shaped like trees, cherries, stars, lemons, or the State of Washington. They came in ten different shades, ten different scents. Once I'd arranged them all by color, I'd sit back at the counter and just look at them for a while, feeling like an itch very deep down somewhere in my brain was finally getting properly scratched.

"Why don't I show you how to do your makeup," Elna replied. Before I could answer, she trotted into the back and returned a minute later with a purple drawstring pouch. She upended everything inside onto the counter, brushing aside a roll of receipt paper and some pens. Tubes of lipstick slid around. A pan of blush spun on its narrow side like a top.

First, she clipped my hair back from my face with a plastic barrette and wiped my skin off with a harsh-smelling pad that burned the edges of my nostrils. "You have good bone structure," she declared. This absolutely thrilled me. I'd never cared about the bones in my face before, but now they felt more important than anything.

Elna took a lighter out of her pocket and softened the tip of an eye pencil with its flame, like she'd done yesterday at the variety store. It occurred to me that she could have lit her own cigarette outside with the loggers earlier. I didn't know quite what to make of it, but it seemed important, like a lesson, something I should remember if I was going to be a girl. She dragged the stick around my lash line and then smudged it all around with a Q-tip.

"You want to make it look like you've slept in it, but in a sexy way," she explained. I nodded as if that meant anything to me at all. She piled mascara onto my eyelashes and instructed me not to blink. She picked up another pencil and, without softening the wax, brushed it in a line along my eyebrows. "You don't want to push too hard with this one," she said. "Your coloring isn't very dark, so you really don't need too strong of a brow." Elna went on to explain how everyone was a season. "Obviously, I'm a warm autumn. I think you're a neutral summer." She buffed a rosy powder into my cheeks and pinched them a little.

As she worked on me, my eyes fell to the tip jar by the register. I had no idea why we even kept it out. No one dropped anything in it, ever. There were just a couple of pennies at the bottom, and they'd been there for as long back as I could remember, which was as far as 1985, when I was two. My first memory in life was being here in the store, eating sugar cubes directly out of a box by the fistful, while my mother sat on the floor repairing one of the freezer cases, wires splayed out all around her on the linoleum.

"Finished," Elna said. I looked at my reflection in one of her many mirrored compacts. "So cute," she added, squeezing my shoulder. "You're like my own little doll." A warm, bubbly feeling spread into my chest. A glimmer of being wanted.

At that moment, my mother came through the hallway divider. She had her big coat on and a pair of work gloves sticking out of her pocket. Her cheeks were ruddy and shining. She glanced at me while surveying the store, then snapped her gaze back, studying my made-up face. She seemed surprised, and a little amused, and maybe a little uneasy.

She turned then to Elna and said, "This must be your doing."

"Just thought I'd teach her the basics, Aunt Anne." Elna smiled sweetly, cocking her head to the side. My mother gave her a long look. I couldn't tell what she was thinking.

Finally, she turned back to me and said, "Don't fall asleep tonight with all that on your eyes. I don't need you getting conjunctivitis."

"I'm not going to get conjunctivitis," I groaned.

"Don't worry," Elna chimed in. "I'll make sure she washes her face before bed."

"All right then," my mother said. "Listen, Jen and I need to drive to Everett to pick up a new vending machine before someone else grabs it. Can I leave you girls here for a couple hours?"

"It's fine," I said.

"If you have any trouble, you call over to the Arthurs."

"I know," I told her, growing irritated.

Elna placed her arm around me. She cooed, "We'll take good care of everything until you get back." I could feel the warmth of her skin through my sleeve. Her nails dug into my shoulder. Hesitation flickered in my mother's eyes. Outside, just beyond the window, Jen was waiting in her pickup truck. I could see her in the driver's seat, tapping her fingers on the wheel, messing with the radio knobs.

"It's fine," I repeated, my voice tense.

My mother frowned and made her way toward the door. Before leaving, she turned and said, "Don't forget to take the chicken out of the freezer. We're going to have a proper dinner tonight."

Elna kept her arm hooked around me, smiling her sweet smile, until my mother was gone. Then, she leaned her elbows on the counter, relaxing her posture. "Jen must be the other person in the picture," she said, gesturing down past the half-open curtain. "The one in the hall?"

"Yeah."

"How long has she been around?"

"Like, four years," I said.

"And the Arthurs?"

"They're our neighbors that way," I said, pointing toward the back of the house. A row of scraggly salmonberry bushes divided our backyards. My whole life I was told to call them if I was alone and anything went wrong. I'd never needed to. They were a big family, three generations in the one house with extra cousins and nephews coming and going all the time. Someone was always puttering around. I'd been left there occasionally when I was small, to be watched whenever my mother needed to run an errand without me. I could remember wandering away from the other kids and going into their cellar, which was dark and cool and contained many rows of shelves with home-preserved food. I used to run my fingers along them, peering up into jars full of tomatoes and cubed beef and peas, my reflection bent and distorted in the glass.

Elna took a tube of pink gloss from her satchel and smoothed the wand over her lips. "You and your mother don't get along?" she asked.

"She pisses me off all the time lately," I muttered.

Elna let out a giggle. She packed the lip gloss back into the bag and turned to me. "Why's that?"

"I don't know," I said. "A lot of things." Really, it was the way I'd catch her frowning at me when I sat at the table doing my homework or eating, like something was bothering her. And the way she'd never tell me what it was, always shaking her head and muttering for me not to forget to take the coins out of the laundry machines, or to remember to put new receipt paper in the till, even though I knew that wasn't what she was really thinking at all. It was how she'd begun to come up with ways to blame me for how other people treated me. More and more, it seemed, she did that. Like there was something I could be doing to get my teachers to like me or to have friends at school but I was just refusing to.

I started to notice the friction between us when I was twelve. My first period came, then the need for a bra, plus six extra inches all in my legs and feet, and a rift between my mother and I that seemed to just appear one morning, narrow but unmistakable. The two of us standing on either side of it, dumbfounded, unsure of what to say. Everything began to shift. The things about me that adults passed off as quirky or maybe even cute just a few years earlier were now off-putting, jarring. Strange, especially for a girl. All the time I spent studying for the geography bee, something they used to praise, had come under scrutiny. *Is that healthy?* my mother had begun to ask me. I'd heard her whisper the word *obsessive* on the phone to someone just a few weeks earlier. Writing to consulates for flags, even, had begun to raise eyebrows and elicit looks of chagrin. It was like the approach of my womanhood tipped the scale of everyone's tolerance, like the glare of an adult life emerging on my horizon had cast the truth of me in a harsh and unlovable light. And it was up to me, it seemed, to do something about it—to make myself more easily digestible, to make everybody comfortable. I noticed my hands were clenched on the sides of the register. Knuckles white and strained.

"Let me guess," Elna said, unwrapping a candy bar from the shelf in front of the till. "The kind of shit that was adorable when you were a little kid is now the same shit that weirds people out now that you've got these." She reached over and gave a quick, hard slap to my chest. I felt a hand-shaped sting radiate over my skin, then fade.

I stared at her, stunned. "How do you know that?"

"Lucky guess," she muttered. Her mouth was full of chocolate and caramel.

"Did my mother say something to you?"

"No," Elna scoffed. "Definitely not." She shook her head, finishing off the rest of the bar and tossing the wrapper into the trash bin beneath the counter. "You two just aren't really all that mysterious."

I watched as she stood up, smoothing down her skirt, before grabbing a box cutter from the shelf beneath the counter and going over to the air freshener package, slashing it open with a loud tear. "Over there, right?" She pointed toward the far wall.

"Yeah," I said. I was surprised she knew where we kept the box cutter. She hadn't even dug around for it, just reached her hand in and slipped it out without looking. I wondered if she'd come out of her room last night, after I'd gone to bed.

She started hanging each sachet on a peg, putting all the lemon ones in a row, then all the cherry on the next peg. They weren't hanging straight. I could see the corners of their plastic wrapping, all uneven. Without turning around, she said, "Are you going to like, trip if I put these in the wrong order?"

"No," I said. "I don't care."

"Right," she muttered, a hint of a smile in her voice. Normally, I'd want to get up and help, if not just do it myself. I didn't like the feeling of sitting there, idle-handed. And she *was* putting them in the wrong order. I hated it. But more than I hated it, I was frozen in place. Mesmerized, kind of. I wanted to hear what she had to say.

"I get what's going on with you and Anne because it was the same deal for me, when I was around your age," Elna said.

"What do you mean?"

"People just lose it when little girls start to grow up." She sat down on the floor in front of the display, leaning against the wall and stretching her legs out in front of her. She had on a pair of platform boots. Dark blue leather with thick black soles. I hadn't seen this pair of shoes yet. I wondered how many she'd brought with her. I wondered how many she owned. I wanted to see what her closet looked like. And her room, and the pages of her diary, if she kept one. I imagined pausing time with the press of a button and inspecting all her things closely, taking inventory, jotting notes, without anybody watching.

"I mean, obviously it wasn't exactly the way it is with you," Elna went on. "Different stuff. But, I think it's all basically the same, right? How people are with us." Her voice trailed off and she looked out the window. "Any girl," she added, "not just you and me."

I knew what she meant. Even though I felt like I was experiencing girlhood on one side of a wall, peeking over from time to time to see what everyone else was doing, sometimes trying and failing to hoist myself over the ledge, I still knew we were all stuck on the outside of something else. A taller, more imposing wall. Unscalable. None of us were getting to the other side where the boys were, where anger and mischief and bold, unabashed confidence were permissible. Encouraged, really. And if their anger ever went too far, everybody fell over their own feet trying to make excuses and apologies for it. When boys fought, even to the point of bloodying each other, it seemed they were only yanked apart and given a clap on the back. When they shouted and screamed, the shushing they got from adults seemed to have a hint of amusement in it, a streak of approval beneath the admonishment.

I had a lot of anger. I was angry at the way people always told me to relax, to be less sensitive, to grow a thicker skin. If I complained about the way overhead lights made my brain feel like it was getting squeezed in a vise, I was too sensitive. If I sat there, silently enduring it, I was criticized for having a sour look on my face. I was angry about being told to smile more. I was angry about being told my smile wasn't quite right when I *did* smile. I was angry at the feeling of the seam in my socks rubbing against my toes, and then at myself for being bothered by a thing like that, for being as sensitive as people accused me of being. At my male teachers frowning when I raised my hand, but beaming at the slightest level of participation from the boys who played sports. At being made to feel like I had too many questions, the wrong kinds of questions, but then getting notes on my report cards that I'd grown much too quiet in class and needed to speak up more. I was angry at how different everything was for girls.

And how even more different everything seemed to be for me, and never knowing why.

My anger felt like a pit of black tar, sputtering and boiling, just at the bottom of my throat. It grew larger every day. As time went on, I could feel it expanding, encroaching upon the soft parts of me. But I knew better than to let it show too much. Even just a hint was met with harsh disapproval from my teachers, my mother, even other girls. When we were still friends, Julie would bristle at my pointing out how differently the school seemed to treat boys. *You're so dramatic,* she once said. In my last year of junior high, I threw a book at the face of a boy who'd snapped my bra strap each time he passed my desk in study hall, pretending to need the pencil sharpener. I knew that the teacher had seen him do it. I saw her silently noticing. But it was me who got sent to the office to sit quietly for the rest of the day, the old ladies behind the desk casting withering glares my way. It was not the boy's mother who got called, but mine. And when I got home, I could tell my mother was annoyed with me, though she didn't say anything about it. There were so many kinds of reminders that, even if it wasn't said outright, the best thing I could be was mild. Sweet. Yielding. Endlessly tolerant. A fawn nestled in the grass. And so, the anger pit widened even more.

"And I don't think it ever really stops, either," Elna said. "But at least you can turn eighteen and do what you want, right? When you have your own money, no one can tell you anything." She looked at me seriously, and I nodded in agreement, though I'd never really thought about it like that before. She eyed my face for a long time, looking around each part slowly and deliberately, like she was memorizing me. For a moment, she seemed sad, then it passed and a little smile turned up one corner of her lips.

All of my thoughts were starting to make me nervous, so I got up out of my seat and said, "I guess I should go take the chicken out of the freezer."

A few steps down the hall, I turned back to yank the divider curtain all the way shut, wanting to keep the chilly store air out of our rooms, and from the corner of my eye, I caught a glimpse of Elna's hand slipping out of the cash register, a twenty-dollar bill gripped in her fingers. She folded it quickly and pushed it inside her pocket.

6

I could tell right away Elna really knew what she was doing with sewing. Late that afternoon, once the loggers had come back in their trucks and dropped their clothes off, I followed her down into the basement to the laundry room, which had a big table meant for folding. We sat together facing the wall, where there was a poster of orcas and otters and porpoises taped up. Marine life of the Pacific Northwest. It was part of a prize package I'd gotten at my first ever geography bee when I was eight, and I'd promptly used it to cover up a big, jagged hole one of our old boarders had punched—he'd been raging about the dryer, saying it ate all his coins. Normally, we'd just run him a free cycle, but he was already two weeks late on his rent and had racked up forty-five dollars of unpaid credit in the store. My mother told him to pipe down. He took a swing at her, and then the next day she changed the locks to his room while he was out working and left his stuff on the curb. Every time I went down there to collect the coins, I'd look at the hole and feel bothered.

Elna sorted through the men's clothes, inspecting each one for damage and putting a little piece of tape by every rip. Then she got to work. I watched as she passed the needle through the thick woolen sleeves, a metal thimble on her thumb. She was deft and quick, confidently laying out the stitches in impossibly neat rows. So tiny, I could barely tell there'd ever been a tear in the first place.

The smell of sweat and pine sap floated up from the fabric and hovered around us. I counted up all the pieces of laundry and did the math in my head. She'd probably make about twenty-five dollars in total once it was all done. I thought then about what I'd seen earlier, her nicking the cash from our register. I tried to come up with reasons it maybe wasn't what it looked like—she just needed to make change for herself, she was only borrowing it, she thought better of the idea and slipped the bill back in when I wasn't looking. I told myself that even if it was exactly what it looked like, she probably really needed it. And here she was now, doing real work to earn money. I felt a bit queasy and uncertain, but I was also impressed. Not just by her skill with the needle, but the way she'd managed to drum up a little business for herself only a couple days after arriving. Elna was capable. She knew how to get things out of the world. Mineral was a totally foreign place to her, full of strangers, far from home, and still she hadn't seemed to miss a beat since first stepping foot off the bus. She could be dropped just about anywhere, I imagined, and find her way.

I wasn't prone to jealousy. It was a feeling I almost never had. But here in the laundry room, watching her sew, I got a surge of something close to it. Not envy, exactly. More like a longing. Like there was a formula my cousin had cracked that made the world, and the people in it, easy for her to navigate. Like she was getting a better deal out of everything, just by being herself. And if I could only figure out that same formula, things would be better for me, too. Deep down, I had a sense that I simply couldn't be like her no matter how hard I might try. But that didn't stop me from aching for it.

"How did you learn to do this?" I asked. She was quiet for a few moments. I wasn't sure if she was going to answer. Then, "My mom was a costume manager at this big drag queen dinner theater for tourists for a while." Elna paused. "You know what drag queens are, don't you?"

"Yes," I said. "I've seen them on *The Ricki Lake Show*."

"Ricki Lake, huh? Doesn't seem like your kind of thing."

"It's not, really. Sometimes I see it when I'm flipping through the channels."

As Elna worked, she described showing up before opening and eating dinner directly from the kitchen, a plate with a bit of everything they were serving that night. Then, going into the big open dressing area where there was a mending station managed by Candace and another woman named Olga. "I was supposed to be doing my homework at a desk they set up in the corner, but I just didn't care about it and neither did anyone else," Elna said. "Instead, I'd watch the queens do their makeup and then when they went to the stage, I'd stay back and watch what was happening with the sewing. After a while I picked up a lot of their techniques, and then eventually the manager started handing me a little money to mend the costumes, too. I replaced probably a million sequins."

"When did your mom stop working there?"

"When I was about your age. Maybe a little younger."

"What happened?"

"They fired her," Elna said, throwing a perturbed look my way, before turning her focus back to the needle gripped between her fingers. "She was missing too many shifts, just sleeping right through them. I couldn't get her out of bed most of the time." Elna sighed, tossing a mended shirt into the wash pile on the floor. "After a while I tried to go back to see if they'd hire me on my own. They said I was too young, but then I saw Olga with her two teenage daughters working in the dressing room on my way out, so I don't know what their problem was." An angry little sneer passed over her lips and then faded. "So, what do you do for fun?" she asked, quickly adding, "Besides flags or whatever."

"I like to go up to this one lake," I said.

"Really," Elna replied. "With that busted heart of yours?" Her voice came out as a low, sarcastic kind of purr.

"It's fine," I told her. "It doesn't hurt my heart."

She worked quietly for a couple more minutes, then asked, "You sneak out then? I know nobody around here is giving you permission to trek up to any lake."

"I go early in the morning, before anyone's awake, to swim."

"And you really just swim?"

"Yeah," I said.

"You ever meet anyone up there?" Elna asked. I shook my head no.

"Didn't think so." She smirked. Then, a moment later, "Ever think about it?"

"No," I told her, baffled. It wasn't that I didn't get what she was suggesting, but that I couldn't imagine poisoning the sanctity of my time alone in the water with the presence of another person.

"You should come visit San Francisco," she said. "I could introduce you to people."

"Who?" I asked.

"My friends." She shrugged. "Maybe some cute boys your age." She looked at me. "Or girls. Whatever." She sewed another line of stitches. "Could be good to get a break from this place," she said, waving her hand around in front of her, keeping her eyes on the fabric. "See some new things."

"Maybe," I said. I didn't really want to meet anyone, but I didn't want to say no to Elna, and I did like the idea of visiting her in California. Or at least I liked that she was offering it to me, that she wanted me to be there with her.

At that moment, I heard the sound of feet shuffling on the stairs. The skin on the back of my neck prickled. Then, a quick knock on the door as it creaked open. A man's voice said, "Forgot these." Elna's demeanor changed in an instant. Her posture straightened, a pleasant smile spread over her face. She turned around, hand outstretched, accepting a jacket and hat from the man, who had now taken one, two, three wide and wobbly steps into the laundry room. It was Tom. He'd been boarding with us for less than a month. He'd bought a bag of sunflower seeds and some rolling papers from me two weeks earlier. He stayed in the first room on the left, just up the stairs. The jacket and hat both had orange reflective strips sewn on. The kind of thing people, the loggers especially, wore in the winter when dusk fell early to avoid getting hit by a flatbed loaded with timber.

"I'll fix these right up for you," Elna said. Without taking her eyes off Tom, she slid the clothing across the table, up against the rest of the pile. One of the strips was dangling off the hat, threads popping loose along the edges.

Tom took a step back and thanked Elna, making his way toward the door. He had an unsteady gait, and seemed to wince a little as he turned his hip to go around the corner. I thought back to ringing up his purchase the other week, if he'd seemed similarly pained then, and all I could remember was that he looked very tired.

My cousin waited until we heard his steps creaking up the basement stairs, then relaxed her shoulders and mouth. "You want to learn something?" she asked. I told her sure, and she grabbed the hat Tom had just dropped off and placed it, along with a thick needle and a spool of orange thread, in front of me. "Do you know how to thread a needle?" I shook my head no. "Here," she said. "I learned this trick at the drag show." I watched as Elna cut a length of the thread with her teeth, then laid it across the firm ridge of her palm. She took the needle and rubbed the eye across the thread fast, back and forth, like she was trying to start a fire. After a moment, as if by magic, the thread had popped up through the eye in a loop. "Now you try it," she said, undoing the whole thing and placing it in my hand. I copied every movement she'd just made, nervous all the way down to my gut. I thought for sure it wouldn't work for me. It reminded me of a thousand other things demonstrated for me that I just couldn't replicate on command. But then, the thread came through exactly as it had for her. I was relieved. And she didn't even seem surprised, which came as another relief.

"Okay," she said. "Now, bring the needle up through the fabric from the inside." I held the hat in my hands, positioning the orange strip back in its place. The material was thick and rough, a dense woolen knit with wide, heavy seams. It was big, too. Bigger than any hat I'd ever worn. Tom must have an unusually large skull, I thought. But he didn't look much different than any of the others. I decided he was probably pretty average, in reality. It was just that I didn't get up close with a lot of men.

"Hold on, you should probably use a thimble," she said, digging under the table to where she'd stashed her sewing kit. It was a blue fabric-covered binder that zipped all the way around, covered in glittery butterfly stickers. Inside were about a dozen spools of thread, a little pincushion stuck full of shining silver needles, thimbles in a little pouch, a rolled-up measuring tape, and an assortment of beads, zipper pulls, colorful buttons, sequins. "You know how to use one of these?"

"I get the idea of them," I said, placing it on my finger and tapping it on the point of the needle. "So I don't get stuck."

"Exactly."

I wasn't about to say anything to Elna, but sometimes I did like sticking myself with pins on purpose. Not all the time, but whenever things got to be too much. I'd been doing it for years.

It was like I could centralize a massive, swirling cloud of stress and anxiety and frustration into a single, manageable point on my body. The pain was already in my body anyway, I reasoned. Headaches, stomachaches, the weirdly empty pangs in my heart. And a seemingly endless crush of impossibly tangled thoughts and feelings swirling around in my brain, working themselves into even worse, tighter knots, clanging against the sides of my head like a pool ball trapped in a dryer. The prickly and exhausting blur of a day at school, all the sounds and lights and awful smells of it. The way it felt to work up the nerve and energy to say something in class, only for a flurry of snickers to spread around the room afterward. Why shouldn't I find a way to gather it all into one place? Control it, somehow, even just for a little while? I'd usually do it on the bottoms of my feet or on my scalp, under my hair, so that there wouldn't be marks for anyone to notice. I understood it was the kind of thing people would think of as bad. Totally unacceptable and creepy. But really, if it made me feel a bit better, I didn't see what the big deal was.

Patiently, Elna showed me how to work the threaded needle up and over, forming rows of neat little stitches in the right places. We worked side by side and I followed her hands closely with my eyes, turning my gaze quickly back and forth between hers and mine, trying to match the movements. A strand of Tom's hair fell out of the hat and landed on my lap. Scraggly and blond. I could see a split forming at the end. I blew it onto the floor.

7

The chicken was ready around six. The four of us, Elna and me, my mother and Jen, all sat around the table together in a labored silence. My cousin was a new cog in the wheel. None of us knew quite how to integrate her into our daily lives. For myself, it felt like a very bright light beamed out all around her, falling onto me, emphasizing the ways I fell short. My mother, it seemed, struggled to know what to say to Elna. I thought maybe she felt awkward having not seen her for so many years, being so out of touch with everything new about her since she was ten, and now seeing her own life, the store and her little family and her aging self, through the eyes of someone young and unfamiliar. And Jen, I guessed, was trying to figure out how to be the right kind of counterweight between the two of us and this new girl, so unlike anyone in Mineral she may as well have come from another world.

My mother clapped her hands together lightly and said, "Let's eat, then." I could see the chicken had been baked in some kind of mustard sauce. The melted fat separated from the bright yellow gravy, forming an oil slick at the top of the dish. There was a bowl of peas next to it, a slab of butter oozing its way through to the bottom. With my fork, I reached over and lifted the skin off of one of the thighs, dropping it on my plate. I liked the skin, gristle, cartilage, and tendons. But the actual muscle meat held little appeal. My mother glared at me. Lately, she'd been on a crusade to get me to eat differently, saying it was a bad habit to pick things apart the way I did. Peeling the frosting off of my slices of cake, eating only the yolk of an egg, cutting the crusts off bread.

Discreetly, Jen transferred some pieces of cartilage from her plate to mine with a serving spoon. I noticed she kept looking at a blister on her forearm. The skin around it was purplish, raised in a half circle around a flat, shining burn about the size of a nickel. A little atoll of ruined flesh. Jen was a welder, sheet metal for industrial appliances plus emergency repair, and was always showing up with minor injuries on her arms and neck and hands. I'd seen the metal helmet she wore. I thought it looked very important. Like the gear of someone charged with exploring a hostile planet. The gloves, too. Huge and black, impossibly thick rubber. Still, she never left work entirely unscathed.

I really liked Jen. We met her first as a boarder. She came to stay after her house in Mineral had a kitchen fire and took three months to repair. Then, after the damage was fixed, she kept coming around to buy sundries or gas, or just to say hello to my mother. There was a tension in the air whenever they were together. And my mother, who was usually a stern, reserved woman, smiled more when she was around. Giggled, even. Soon, Jen was over for dinner all the time. On my twelfth birthday, she drove the three of us to Pioneer Square in Seattle, where there was a store called Metsker that sold nothing but maps and flags. It was the best place I'd ever seen. I spent a very long time combing through the shelves, carefully calculating what I could get with the money I'd been allotted. They had a large display of regional flags from all around the world, most of which I'd never seen before. To me, the most beautiful one was from a town in Serbia: deep, hypnotic blue with an illustration of a silver moth and a golden cocoon. Jen stood next to me, looking up at it, while I explained why I liked it so much. She did not seem bored. She did not seem to be humoring me. And then she bought me this strange, lovely Serbian flag.

Mostly though, I liked Jen because she was a good listener. She never tried to be overly familiar, never pried with too many questions. She knew she was not my parent. But I never felt like I didn't matter to her. I once came home after a particularly bad day at school and sat down on the back step of the house, distraught, looking out into the Arthurs' yard, keeping my gaze fixed on a rusty old swing set. The cold air did something good to my brain. I could just make out the distant chime of the bell from the inside of the store, somebody opening the shop door, but I didn't move. I couldn't make myself. A few minutes later, Jen was standing next to me on the step.

"You know where your mom's at?" she asked. I didn't say anything. "She go on an errand or something?" Again, I didn't respond. Jen stood there, quietly. I could feel her eyes on the back of my neck. Then she disappeared inside, and I thought she had left, but instead she returned with a pad of paper and a pen, then sat down all the way on the other side of the step, giving me space. She wrote *You okay?* and handed the paper back to me along with the pen.

Moderately, I wrote back.

School?

Yes.

I hated school, too, she wrote.

Takes the juice out of me, I answered. Jen nodded. Using the paper, she asked if I wanted anything from inside. I shook my head no, then took the pen and explained that my mother was out getting her car inspection done in Bellingham. Jen nodded, then wrote, *Going to watch the register for a while, if you're OK with that.* I circled the word *OK,* and she went back inside.

My cousin finished her plate quickly, then speared another piece of chicken from the dish. Between bites, she explained what she was trying to get started in the basement. "A little mending business," she said. "To earn some money while I'm here."

"That's very enterprising of you," my mother replied.

"You know," Elna said, "I'd be happy to fix any of your clothes too, Anne." She looked my mother up and down sweetly, eyes falling over her faded plaid button-down. Pink and yellow stripes, one missing button. Half tucked into a pair of jeans from the previous decade. My mother didn't really care for clothes. She loved poker. She loved cats, though we hadn't had one in a couple years. She read a lot of science fiction novels. She did jigsaw puzzles. Sometimes I'd see her pause while doing something in the yard to look closely at a fallen leaf from our huge old maple tree, bringing it just inches from her face and then holding it up to the sun, letting the light display its many veins.

"That's very nice, Elna, thank you," she said. Her tone was a little curt, I thought.

"Do you maybe know anyone else who could need repairs done?" Elna asked. "Besides the loggers."

"Well, I'm not sure—"

"Anybody in the neighborhood?"

"I suppose one of the Arthurs might need something, possibly," my mother said. "There's usually quite a few people over there." I looked out the window over to their house. It was more like three houses from different times cobbled together: the original old bungalow with its sloped roof; a split-level addition off the back, built in the seventies; and what looked like half of a log cabin stuck onto the side of everything, added over a few weekends one summer when I was a little kid. It was an Arthur family collective effort. I could remember sitting out back watching them construct it, eating Popsicle after Popsicle in the hot sun. They fought and caroused and got mildly injured, and before long the work was finished.

I saw Elna looking out the window, too. There were two cars parked haphazardly in their driveway. I saw shadows moving inside the curtains. "So," Elna said, tapping her fingers on the table and looking to the side. "Any word from my mother?"

"I haven't heard anything," my mother said.

"I know she was supposed to call."

"That's true." A pained look passed over my mother's face. "I'm sure she will soon."

"You're sure you haven't missed it?"

"I really don't think so," she said, her voice now hushed, like she could sneak past her own discomfort, and Elna's, if she were only quiet enough. "I always make sure there's room on the tape." She gestured to the answering machine in the corner by the phone and the Rolodex in its yellowed, plastic dome. The machine was one of the older kinds, with a fake wood–paneled front and a clear window with two cassettes inside. We'd talked about getting a digital one. A lot of people had them. But I knew that until ours broke, we'd keep rewinding the tapes, recording new messages over the old.

"If she doesn't call soon," my mother offered, "we'll dig up the number and see if we can just reach her there."

"Sure," Elna said. She gave a little shrug. On the surface, it seemed like she didn't care all that much. But I could tell she only wanted to *look* as though she didn't care about it. My mother began chewing on her lip, which was something she did whenever she had nerves. And Jen, watching everything quietly until that moment, cleared her throat and asked whether anyone was interested in seeing the movie *Titanic*, which had finally arrived at the nearest theater, about an hour away, and which we almost never went to. Elna said that she'd already seen it, and then the table was quiet again.

. . .

Later that night my mother and I sat out on the back steps in our down jackets, watching the snow flurries. She was smoking one of her long, skinny cigarettes. Each week she pulled one pack from the shelf behind the register. The cartons were wrapped in either pink or mint foil, and labeled with loopy, girlish cursive. *My slims,* she called them. I didn't usually come out on the porch with her when she smoked before bed, but she'd called me out there while I was in the kitchen getting a glass of water.

"You and your cousin appear to be getting on," she said. I nodded. "So," she pressed, "how's she seem?"

"Seem?"

"I mean, do you think she's doing all right?"

"I think so."

"She gave me a hand with the dishes and mentioned you were helping her out with the mending." She used the glowing stub of her first cigarette to light a new one. "And that you learned a little yourself. I didn't know you were interested in sewing."

"I'm not, really."

"But you like spending time with Elna?"

I did like hanging around Elna. I liked watching her, the way she carried herself in the world. How she knew what to say to people. I liked her doing my makeup. I didn't so much like the stealing. Especially at the variety store, where we could be caught by the owner and thrown out and possibly dealt with by the police. But in a way, I kind of did like the stealing, too. I didn't want to explain any of this to my mother, so I just said, "I guess."

"You two have nice talks?"

"She's only been here a few days," I said, annoyed. I felt like a bug pinned to a board. "But yeah, our talks are nice. I don't know."

"Well." She sighed. "It's a good sign the girl's doing something productive. My sister's done a real number on her, I'm sure."

"Why hasn't Candace called?" I asked.

"It's hard to say." She let out a long, tired breath. "Maybe she can't use the phone there yet. Maybe she forgot. Maybe she put the number in wrong."

"Elna said she's been to these places a lot of times."

"Rehab? That's true."

"Why haven't we ever visited her?" I asked.

"You have school." My mother packed her slims and the lighter into a small pouch, which she zipped into the pocket of her coat. Fluffy bits of snow drifted to the ground and then melted in an instant. The moon sat tall in the sky. A thin, bright crescent. "I did visit once," she said. "When she was at a place outside Sacramento." I listened as she described taking a wrong exit off the Five and driving miles and miles through almond plantations before arriving, not long before the end of visiting hours, at a big white building in the desert. "Candace had a miniature harp in her room, somehow," my mother explained, raising her hand up about three feet to show me the height of the instrument. She described watching her sister sit by the window, gently strumming the harp over and over. I could picture her easily. Her blond hair backlit by the desert sun, soft music flowing from her hands. In my mind, she wore a gauzy white gown.

"When?" I asked.

"When you were a baby."

"So, you took me with you."

"What else could I do?" she said. "You were so small."

"Where was Elna?"

"Staying with a neighbor, I think."

"I don't remember it at all."

"Of course you don't. You weren't even one year." She looked at her hands, clasped in her lap. She chewed on her lip. Then she said, "Time for you to go to bed." She stood up and opened the door to the kitchen, pointing me inside.

8

The next day, I went to check the answering machine for any word from Candace. I felt bad all night thinking about the disappointed look on Elna's face. I'd always been a terrible sleeper. There were many nights I'd wake up every hour and then just lie there, thoughts racing. Even if nothing bad happened during the day, there was a strong chance I'd wind up with my eyes wide open at three in the morning. It was like my brain simply couldn't shut all the way off. I couldn't control it. I'd get obsessed with something, like imagining the many fine hairs on a spider's legs, or the sound of a particular word, and the next thing I knew my alarm was beeping.

I yawned, brushing a single, shriveled pea from last night's dinner from the counter to the floor. The kitchen was empty. Frost crept up the window behind the sink. It didn't look like much snow had stuck, though. I could see blades of grass, still green, poking up through the patio steps.

I found the yellow light blinking on the machine, but the message wasn't from Candace. It was the school guidance counselor. I recognized his voice immediately. I grabbed the volume dial and turned it down right away, anxious that someone would hear. I knew my mother was out in the store—I could hear her cleaning the floor, the rusty groan of the mop bucket getting dragged around. I hadn't seen any sign of Elna yet.

Hello, Ms. Robinson, the counselor said. I could hear voices in the background, a door opening, another phone ringing. *I'm calling in regard to our last conversation about the uh . . .* I heard him mutter the words *yes, no,* and *half and half, please. Sorry about that,* he said. He slurped something from a cup. Then, *The alternative program, I have more information. Please return my call at your convenience.*

My chest felt cold and tight. This wasn't the first time I'd heard something about a program. A while ago I'd eavesdropped on one side of a conversation between the two of them, here in the kitchen, by staying quietly inside the pantry after the phone rang while I was in there looking for my lunch bag. I heard the words *skill building,* and *reinforcement,* something about using the time when I sat out of gym. But that was in early fall, and nothing had come of it. I deleted today's message and wound the tape back, keeping a potholder pressed over the machine to dampen the whirring sound.

The counselor's name was Mr. Carter and I'd already met with him many times. His office smelled like onions and cleaning fluid. It was located in the corridor that joined the junior and senior high schools. He was friendly, but not in a real way, not like Jen. He smiled too much and made a lot of jokes. I got the sense he believed I never laughed because I didn't understand them, but really, I just didn't think they were funny.

I was first sent to him three years ago, in the sixth grade, by a teacher who had many problems with me. I wasn't sure exactly what finally did it. I remember thinking about it as I walked down the hall, pass in hand, all the things I'd recently gotten in trouble over. I couldn't hold a pencil the right way. I didn't believe there *was* a right way to hold a pencil and put up a stubborn fight about it with this teacher. I hadn't managed to learn how to tie my shoes, either, so if I wore ones with laces and they came undone before the end of the day I'd sometimes take them off and go sock-footed in the hallway, which she also hated. Sometimes I made my own modifications to homework assignments or projects, if I thought they weren't challenging or interesting enough. The teacher told me they weren't *suggestions,* they were requirements. I told her that was a fine opinion to have, but I didn't need to share it.

Mr. Carter was waiting for me by his door with a big, wet grin, announcing that he'd set up a weekly meeting for us. He tried to get me to play games with him. Checkers, Battleship, Guess Who?, nothing I ever cared about. And he'd try to get me to talk about my life. I never knew what to tell him.

"It must be tough not having a father around," he once said.

"No, it really isn't," I replied. He made a pinched-up face at me in response, like he'd gotten an awful taste in his mouth. Like

I was supposed to feel really sad about not having a father, and there was something offensive about the fact that I simply didn't.

The fifth time I was sent to him, my mother was there. I was surprised to see her sitting in one of the worn plastic seats in front of his desk. She held her purse, which was also worn, tightly in her lap like she needed something to hang on to, and gave me only a quick glance as I came through the doorway. I sat next to her, confused, waiting. She checked her watch a couple times and then glanced at me again, this time letting her eyes fall on my leggings, which I was wearing inside out, so the seams and tags wouldn't touch my skin.

Mr. Carter cleared his throat and declared, "Young Ida's just a square peg in a round world." He said this to my mother only, like I wasn't even there, leaning back against his chair and smiling from the other side of the desk. He had the satisfied look of someone who'd just finished a three-thousand-piece puzzle. I wished he were made of paper, so I could crumple him up and throw him in the wastebasket. He kept talking, but in my mind I went somewhere else completely.

I was sent out of his office for the last twenty minutes, while he and my mother spoke privately. I had a sick feeling sitting there in the hallway on the bench. A feeling of having done something wrong, and everyone could understand what it was but me. On the way home she said, "Of course I know you're a square peg. But what the hell are we supposed to do about it?"

"I don't think we need to do anything," I muttered.

She was quiet for a minute, then said, "This guy just gets paid to make the same observations any parent with half a brain cell could." She seemed mad. I noticed she was gripping the steering wheel tightly, biting her lip. "You need to do what your teachers tell you, all right?" Her voice was tense, bordering on angry. "I can't be running back and forth to the school like this. I don't know what to tell them anymore. Just start acting the way you're supposed to."

"What do you mean back and forth?" I asked. "When else have you been there?"

"A few times," she muttered.

"A few times?" I repeated. "Since when?"

"They first asked me to come in when you were in second grade." She gave me a quick sideways glance. I stared at her. "And then several times since then."

"How many is several?"

"I don't know, exactly, Ida." She sighed.

"How can you not know?"

"Look, it doesn't matter, you don't need to worry about it." She shook her head, exasperated. "What you need to worry about is starting to mind your teachers. I know you're smart, I know you understand the difference between good and bad behavior, so you need to start trying harder." We stopped at a red light and I leaned my head against the window. The air was clear enough to see Mount Baker on the horizon. Wispy clouds hovered around the peak. I wished I could trade places with one of them. I wished I could be up there in the cold, silent air. I'd have rather been even a single droplet of rainwater, suspended in the troposphere, falling to earth and evaporating over and over again, than live another day inside my body. We drove on.

"You never told me the school was asking you to come in," I muttered, crossing my arms.

"I don't have to tell you things," she clipped. "I'm your mother, not your friend." We spent the rest of the way home in strained silence.

After deleting the message, I sat down at the kitchen table and pulled my sweater over my knees, wrapping my arms around my legs. I glared at the answering machine, tears stinging at my eyes. I could hear my mother wringing the mop out down at the other end of the hall, water dripping into the bucket. The sound of the door chime, and then a few minutes later the till opening and shutting. I closed my eyes and imagined I was at Needle Lake, plunging beneath the water. Weightless and invisible to the world aboveground. The confines of gravity gone, the pinprick of the sun growing smaller and smaller beyond the rippling surface. When I opened my eyes, I saw Elna through the window walking across the yard toward the house, her red hair beaming in the daylight. She was holding a paper sack in her hands. She hopped up the three patio steps and opened the door, letting in a burst of cold air. Her cheeks were red and shining.

"What's that?" I asked, pointing to the bag.

"I went over to your neighbors' place," she said, looking back toward the fence that divided our yard from the Arthurs'. "They gave me some stuff to work on." She pulled out a small quilt. One of the squares had come apart. Eight diamond-cut flaps of calico fabric falling limp around a puff of stuffing. "Bunch of weirdos over there," she muttered. "That guy with the blond beard, Patrick?" I nodded. He was a nephew who'd been around a lot over the last year. My mother said he was kicked out of the military. I'd seen him in the backyard, shooting cans off the roof with a BB gun. He'd never bothered me. Sometimes I'd look out the window and see him just sitting in his car, bobbing his head along to music in the driver's seat. Elna stuffed the quilt back in the bag. "He came out of nowhere and asked me if I'd ever read the Book of Job."

"Have you?" I asked.

"No," she said, squinting at me. "Then some old woman gave me this dress with a busted zipper." She pulled out what looked like a child's Communion gown. White taffeta, yellowing at the seams. A row of satin flowers around the waist. It looked like it was from another time. I remembered a story about the oldest generation of the family, the grandparents, having a daughter who died at the age of nine. "Anyway," Elna said, putting the bag on the floor. "What's wrong with you?"

"What do you mean?"

"You look upset."

"I'm fine," I told her.

"You don't look fine."

I picked at a loose thread on my sweater for a few moments, unsure of how to explain it. She asked me again what was wrong, so I told her about the message. Then I found myself telling her about going to the counselor's office, how much I hated having to sit there while he took notes about me that I was never allowed to see. How I didn't know exactly what this special program was, but I didn't like the sound of it. She leaned back, listening with her arms crossed. She didn't try to busy herself with anything else while I spoke, didn't have the look of wandering thoughts behind her eyes. She just sat there, nodding.

When I was finished, she said, "You want me to call the school and find out what's going on?"

"They're not going to tell you anything," I scoffed. "They have no idea who you are." She looked at me then like I was the dumbest person in the world and said, "I'm going to say I'm your mother. They'll tell me exactly what they would tell her." I stared in disbelief. "Trust me," she said. "I'm really good at this."

We stood together at the phone table while I punched in the number. Before pressing the last button, I listened for the sound of the mop bucket dragging around the store and didn't hear it.

"What if my mother walks in while you're talking to them?" I whispered.

Elna shook her head. "I saw her walking around the front with a hose and a sponge. I think she's washing the windows." She took the receiver from me and held it between her shoulder and cheek, picking some lint off her shirt. "What's the guy's first name?" she asked.

"Bill," I said. I imagined the call moving through the phone lines, a blip shooting along the wires on our street, up the roadway rumbling with logging trucks, before landing at the school, which was situated on a defunct lumber field. There were still old stumps dotting the grass around the blacktop, and a rusty wood chipper left to the elements near the bus entrance. I knew winter break didn't mean the school just sat empty. We'd driven past it during holiday closures and saw that the parking lot was still half full of the same cars I saw teachers and office workers getting out of during the rest of the year.

Elna twirled the phone cord around her fingers. I noticed she'd repainted her nails. Thick, glittery blue. When the school picked up, everything about her demeanor changed, just like it had when Tom came into the basement. She straightened her back and put on a bland smile, like a woman in a detergent commercial. She placed her hand on her hip. When her voice came out of her mouth, it sounded different. Older. Confident. Eerily similar to my mother's. "This is Anne Robinson returning Bill Carter's call."

The conversation went on for about ten minutes. There were a lot of pauses, a lot of sounds of acknowledgment and understanding from Elna. She kept going *Mm-hmm,* and staring up at the ceiling, rolling her eyes. I got the sense she was not impressed with Mr. Carter, which reassured me. She asked a few questions, and ended the call with a simple *I'll think about it and be in touch.* I was impressed by the *in touch.* It sounded so authentically middle-aged.

She set the phone down and turned to the fridge, opening the door and pulling out a gallon of chocolate milk, taking a long series of gulps directly from the bottle. I hated that her lips were touching the plastic. I made a note in my head to never pour a drink from this container again, because it had been irreversibly tainted, but I didn't say anything aloud. She wiped her mouth with her sleeve.

"Well, it's what you thought," she said, her voice now back to normal. "They want to put you in some special class during gym and recess."

"Where?"

"In the school, I think. That guy is running it. The counselor." She rolled her eyes again. "You should just drop out," she added.

"I can't drop out of school," I said, baffled and a little annoyed at the suggestion. It didn't make sense. It wouldn't be possible. Elna stared at me, one brow raised, the hint of a smile on one corner of her mouth. Just then, just for a moment, I noticed a little bit of curiosity creeping over the edge of my irritation. A quick flash of intrigue.

"Well," Elna went on, "it's bullshit. Isn't that when you study your maps or whatever? You told me you go to the library."

"Yeah."

"I never heard of a school trying to keep a kid out of the library," she said. "That would never happen at the school I went to at home. They would love you there."

"Really?" Another quick flash of interest passed over me.

"Yeah," she said, nodding. "Definitely."

"Well." I looked at the ground. "Did he say anything else about it?"

"Um." She drummed her fingers on the table. "Something about interpersonal skills. Communication practice." She got up and took a piece of white bread from the bag on the counter, folding it into a compact square, and ate it in a single bite.

I thought I might throw up. Not because of the bread, but just the idea of having to be in a room with this man every day after winter break, him telling me how to speak. I knew he would want me to work on my tone. Adults were constantly telling me the problem wasn't what I said, it was *how* I said it. I didn't understand how speaking to me in riddles was any better. I knew he was going to try to get me to hold a pencil differently. He was probably going to wrap his hand around mine, manipulating my fingers and forcing my wrist to move over the page, practicing writing out sentences with the pencil controlled by my index finger, instead of the way I was used to holding it, which was in sort of a four-fingered grip.

The only part of school I didn't hate was my time alone in the library. It was quiet, and half the lights were broken so it wasn't as bright as the hallways or classrooms, and the librarian never spoke to me. No one bothered me in there, because hardly anyone went in there, and the tables were big enough for me to spread out large maps without any part of the paper hanging off the edge. I couldn't imagine going a whole day in that building without any time to myself. I couldn't imagine trading the silent escape of the library for some man in a sweater vest telling me to smile. Thinking of it made me so upset I slapped my hand down on the table before I could stop myself. Elna looked up from reading the label on the chocolate milk. She seemed only mildly surprised, and went right back to looking at the jug. My shoulders relaxed. That was part of what I liked about her. She didn't seem to care much how I acted. We sat quietly for a few minutes while she finished the rest of the milk.

Finally, she picked the bag up from the floor and said, "Want to help me with this?"

9

For the next few nights, I followed Elna down into the basement and sat at the table learning to make tiny, even stitches. Sometimes pine needles or loose dirt fell from the clothes. Sometimes a phone number scrawled on a scrap of paper, or a lighter, or a piece of beef jerky. Once the repairs were done, we loaded everything into the machines. I liked sitting there with her as they tumbled and whirred, warm air swirling all around us and the powdery scent of fabric softener lingering in the air.

We talked about all kinds of things. She told me stories about boyfriends she'd had. A construction worker who'd survived a fall off the Golden Gate Bridge. "Or so he claimed," Elna said. A guy who gave her a pair of real diamond earrings. One who worked at the zoo and brought her in after closing to feed a steak to a tiger with her bare hands. She told me about eating a tequila worm on a beach in Mexico with Candace and one of Candace's friends, who was now dead, but had been Miss Arizona in 1983. She told me about skipping school to watch surfers at Ocean Beach with her friends.

I felt like she had begun to think of me as a friend. We were becoming close in the way I saw in movies. Two girls, enmeshed. Everything she told me, I wanted to know more about. I asked her to draw a map of the apartment she lived in with Candace, just a simple box outline on paper, so I could imagine everything she was describing. I asked her to tell me about her room, cataloging in my mind all the details about her closet and her CD rack and where she kept her many shoes lined up in a row. One night, she took her bracelet off and gently slipped it onto my wrist. Sparkly, lavender beads with a silver butterfly charm in the middle. No one had ever done anything like that before. I felt a surge of belonging so powerful I thought my heart might explode in my chest.

Another night, she braided my hair into a complicated twist down the back of my neck. While she worked at it, I listened to her tell me about going to a rock concert and kissing the singer on the mouth when he came out into the audience. I wanted to hear all about what she wore.

At the end of the week, while we were sitting at the makeshift sewing table, Elna said, "You ask a lot of questions."

"Sorry," I muttered.

"It's okay."

"Does it bother you?"

"No, it's just that I haven't heard a whole lot about you," she said. A nervous flutter rippled through my stomach. I knew I was supposed to talk, but I wasn't sure what to tell her. She asked me if I'd heard from Mr. Carter, the counselor, and I told her no. She asked me if I was worried about it and I told her that I was.

Then, I found myself blurting out something that had happened last year on the school bus. I'd never told anyone else about it. It almost seemed like a bad dream I'd had, instead of something that was real. Five kids, two boys and three girls, called me to the back few rows, where I never usually sat. I remembered the bus rumbling beneath my boots as I walked toward them, the smell of the driver's cigarette and the cool air from the open window, her long, bleached braid swinging over the back of her seat, her green acrylic nails tapping on the wheel, her collection of Grateful Dead bobblehead bears arranged in a rainbow on the dashboard.

Describing it to Elna, I felt like I was watching it from above, like a ghost floating near the ceiling. There I was, sitting down in one of the bench seats while all five faces looked at me with inscrutable smiles. And then five pairs of hands, grabbing me and slamming me, face up, onto the floor behind the seatback, holding me down, the floor caked in mud tracks from snow boots and littered with loose pencils and candy wrappers. The vibration of the wheels moving over the road rattling my skull. And then one pair of hands reaching down to my face and clamping down over my mouth and nose, squeezing so hard no air could get in. My body tried to thrash. The minutes passed, and my vision went black, and a burning feeling like a fast fire spread in my lungs, desperate for air. Julie, the girl who used to come over after school and sit with me at lunch, looked at me from a seat across the aisle, quiet, like she was watching a TV show. I explained all of this to Elna in one long burst. When I was finished, my palms felt cold and damp and my heart was pounding.

My cousin looked at me for a long time, her eyebrows pushed together, and then finally said, "That's pretty fucked up, Ida."

"I know."

"No wonder you don't want to go back to school."

"Well, I stopped taking the bus."

"You're just walking all the way there?"

"It's not that far. I like to walk."

"Must get cold."

"I really don't mind the cold," I said.

"You didn't tell anyone what happened?"

"No," I told her.

"And your fucking friend just sat there, watching." Elna shook her head like she'd gotten a taste of something awful in her mouth.

"She wasn't my friend anymore by then."

"Julie wasn't really your friend *ever*," Elna replied. She opened the dryer door and pulled out a mountain of hot clothes. We began to fold them at the table, separating them into piles. I thought about what she said, about Julie never really being my friend. It wasn't an idea that had ever occurred to me before, but now I couldn't get it out of my head, even though I wanted to. "You know," she said. "I wasn't kidding about school being better for you in San Francisco."

"What do you mean?"

"It would just be different there. They wouldn't be after you all the time about the way you talk, or whatever. You could keep sitting out recess and gym every day and do your maps." She looked at me. "The library is really big. I bet it has even more maps than here."

"It probably does," I said. "Our selection is pretty small."

"And I'd be around," she added. "I could look out for you."

"But you dropped out, though."

"Doesn't matter. I'd make sure nobody fucked with you." She patted me on the knee. "You could come back with me and check it out," she said. "Just something to think about."

Once we finished folding the piles, Elna got started on the Communion dress. She'd been putting it off all week. The quilt was already done, mended and ready to go back next door. I could tell she was annoyed to be fixing the zipper. She pushed the needle in and out of the fabric in a fast huff, gripping the dress like it might run away. "I don't know why she even gave this to me," Elna said, frowning. "I seriously doubt anyone's going to wear this again. It's been sitting in a box for probably thirty years." She brought it up to her face and sniffed, then dropped it down with a look of disgust. A moment later, she sneezed. "Will you return these?" she asked. "I don't want to talk to that weird guy again if I can help it."

"Sure," I said.

I reached out and touched one of the satin rosettes, running my fingers along the folds of a petal and wondering if it had belonged to the dead Arthur girl, and if they'd left her room intact with her other clothes still in it, and if they thought of her less and less as time went on or if she was still on their minds all the time.

While Elna was folding the dress back into its bag, Tom appeared in the doorway. He had on a stained T-shirt and a pair of pajama pants with red hearts on them. Shadows of stubble inched up from his neck. He paused in the doorway, looking at the marine mammal poster that covered the hole punched in the wall, then approached the table.

"Hi, Tom," Elna said, smiling like she'd known him forever. "Here to pick up?"

"Yeah," he replied. "But I don't have any cash right now."

"No?" Elna said.

"I should be getting some tomorrow."

"Then you can pick up your pants tomorrow."

"I don't have another warm pair like that," Tom said. "We're supposed to get snow overnight." He shifted from foot to foot, looking uncomfortable. Elna put down the shirt she was working on and looked at him for a long moment. I could see her thoughts churning like a fast machine. Her tongue darted out of her mouth for a fraction of a second and moved over her lip.

"All right," she said. "You can owe me." She slid the pants across the table. Tom took them without a word and made his way back up the stairs, pausing on the landing and hunching over for a second before moving on.

Once he was out of sight, Elna said, "That guy's hooked on painkillers."

"What? How do you know?"

"Well, he walks weird. That's the first thing."

"He just has a bad leg," I said.

"Well yeah, exactly. I heard Charlie telling one of the other boarders about Tom having an accident at his last job in Idaho. They put steel in his leg, but they fucked it up and had to do it over."

"A lot of them get hurt," I said. "It's a pretty dangerous job. Things happen all the time."

"Yeah, but it's the way he moves. Like his stomach hurts all the time. He's always pressing his hand on his pocket and touching something in there. He's moody. He's got this glassy look in his eye." She shook her head and threaded a new needle, pulling the string out before her and knotting it deftly with one hand. "And he's out of cash before payday? He's spending it on pills."

"I guess it's possible," I said.

"Trust me. I know how to spot it." A dark look passed over her face.

"Well then maybe he won't have five dollars for you tomorrow," I said. "If you're right about him."

"That's okay," Elna said, shrugging. "We'll figure something out."

10

When I went to return the quilt and the dress the next day, I found Patrick standing out in the driveway with his hands in his pockets, looking at something near the gutter. "Do you know what that is?" He pointed a long, skinny arm toward the corner where the grass met the garage door.

"No," I told him. All I could see was a small hole surrounded by a little mound of dirt. It wasn't wider than a Ping-Pong ball.

"That's a king snake nest."

"How do you know?"

"I saw one this morning, squeezing a mouse." He turned his face toward the sun, squinting. "Red on black, friend of Jack."

I tried to picture a king snake. I'd read about them, in a book about reptiles of the Northern Pacific. He was right that they weren't venomous to humans. "Red on yellow, kills a fellow," I said, finishing the rhyme. He let out a big whoop, like he was cheering on a horse race. "Here's your stuff back," I said, handing him the bag. He took it and set it down on the hood of his car, then reached into his pocket, pulling out eight dollars in ones. I tucked the money into my jacket.

"Name a country that starts with the letter Y," he said.

"Yemen."

He lifted his head to the sky and let out a loud cackle, slapping his hand on his thigh and grinning. His teeth were not very white. The hair on his face was reddish blond, growing down from his cheeks into a scraggly patch of a beard. Still laughing, he said, "I heard you were good at that. Give me another one."

"There are no other Y's," I said.

"Z."

"Zambia, Zimbabwe."

"You're a funny kid," he said.

I didn't know what to say, so I said, "There's only one O name, too. Oman."

"That so?"

"Yes. And only one Q. Qatar."

"You ever think about going to any of these places you read about?" He took a loose cigarette out of his coat and lit it, his hand sheltering the flame from the cold wind.

"All the time," I said, surprising myself. I never really talked to anybody about the things I wanted. Before he'd asked me, it didn't even feel like the daydreams meant anything real. Just foggy visions of distant places I'd touched on maps. My imaginings made up of every grainy picture I'd seen printed in a book, every clip of video I'd watched on a screen, a shaky collage of the world filtered all the way down to me through other people's lives. I realized suddenly that I wanted very much to go to the Raja Ampat archipelago. I saw part of a documentary on PBS about it, where they took underwater cameras down into the ocean. Black-and-white-striped sea snakes, fluttering like long ribbons against the brightest blue. Schools of shimmering rainbow fish turning and flitting around masses of brilliant coral. A giant clam, six feet long.

"I always have a feeling about things. I have a way with that," Patrick said, his face obscured by a cloud of smoke. "And I believe you will go to all kinds of places outside of this pockmark." He spat the word *pockmark* out, almost shouting it, his free hand thrusting violently before him in a sudden punch, like he was trying to push the entire town of Mineral into another plane of existence. The smoke around his face dissipated. He composed himself, taking a delicate pull on his cigarette, then added, "But first, I don't think things will be too good for you. Not for a while." He put the cigarette out on the asphalt, then got up close to the snake hole and crouched down, peering into it with his hands cupped over his eyes.

"All right. Let me know if you want anything else fixed," I said, turning to make my way back to the other side of the fence. When I reached my yard, I could still see him there, waiting for something to emerge from the nest.

I stood there and watched him for a while longer, then zipped my jacket all the way up to the chin and walked past the edge of the property, hands stuffed in my pockets. The day was cold and bright. I kept going down the street, turning at the corner onto one of the old logging roads that cut through the woods. No trucks came down it anymore after the main way had been paved and connected to the highway and all the worksites. Deep tire grooves still remained in the mud, now half frozen. Loose pieces of timber that fell off flatbeds years ago cut across the path every so often, their carcasses all covered in moss. Some had small trees, no thicker than my thumb, beginning to grow from them.

The road circled widely around Mineral, connecting at one point to the trail I took up to Needle Lake and to the other trail that went up the backside of the mountain, where a new lumber allotment was getting established. Sometimes I just walked on it for no real reason. No purpose other than being alone in a quiet place. Sometimes I'd go a little ways off the path and sit down in the wooded area, my back against a tree. I'd sit still enough for so long that animals would begin to emerge, unwary of my presence. White-tailed deer, rabbits, bluebirds. I saw a fox trot by once with something small hanging out of its mouth. Another time I dozed off and woke up to the orange glow of the sun setting over the tree line.

As I walked, I thought about what Patrick had said. He was just my neighbors' nephew, he didn't know anything about me. But still, there was a part of me that felt he was right. Not because I trusted him or thought he was wise. I didn't. But because I also felt like I was moving toward something dark. I'd once overheard my mother saying to Jen, *It's like she can't let happiness rise all the way up to the top of her head.* They were both tipsy, sitting on the back steps on a summer weekend. If I hadn't been eavesdropping,

I would've corrected her. It wasn't that I didn't want to let it rise. More that there was something on the other end of it, weighing it down. A boulder tied to the end of a rope. I felt like I was always fighting with it, struggling to break free. Somewhere down in my gut I had the sense that one day I would, and that I would glide over sparkling blue waters, mapping the hidden parts of the world. But first, the heaviness.

I walked for a long time. Clouds passed over the sun. It rained for a few minutes, then stopped, then a flurry of snowflakes drifted down over the muddy grass. My brain grew quieter the farther I walked. My thoughts divided from one burning, frantic mass into separate fragments. Each one distinct from the other, gently spinning in their own corner of the mind, like leaves floating on a pond. As the minutes passed, the thoughts grew thinner and lighter. I picked them up one by one and blew them into the wind. I pretended I *was* the wind, and that I didn't have a body. I imagined what it would be like to never go home. I imagined what it would be like to not be a girl. I ran for a while, as fast as I could, ignoring my heart twinging in my chest. If I was the wind, I wouldn't have a heart at all. I wouldn't go to the doctor, or need to eat. No one could call my name, because I wouldn't have one. I would be gone in an instant.

Eventually, I came to a small clearing half grown over with brush. It was where the trucks used to connect to the main street through town. A rusty signpost with the number 10 on it remained, ivy creeping up the pole. Salmonberry and hawthorn bushes had begun to take over, forming a barrier over the entrance. I crouched in the brush, catching my breath. Through the openings, I could see cars and people. A fire hydrant. The variety store, the shoe store, a big black dog with a red leash walking alongside a man. Someone dropped a brown paper bag on the ground. A sack of apples and a loaf of bread tumbled out. I watched them bend over to pick everything up. I counted three blue cars and two silver ones go by. A group of kids my age came out of the store and huddled together at the corner. I could hear their murmured laughter drifting over, making its way across the street and into the bushes. I stayed there for a while, unseen, my fingers growing numb in the cold air, just watching the day happen to people, before turning around and going back home.

11

I came back in through the front entrance, unzipping my coat in the hallway that separated the store from the apartments. My lips felt cold and rubbery. I brought my hands to my face and tried to press some warmth back into my cheeks. Through the window panel on the shop door, I could see my mother slowly making her way around the aisles with a clipboard, taking the monthly inventory. Her lips moved as she counted up what was left of each product, writing the number on the sheet, marking a big circle around the things that needed to be reordered. She had her portable cassette player clipped to the waistband of her jeans and an old pair of taped-up headphones over her ears. I was sure she was listening to the Allman Brothers. She was always trying to get me to listen to them, too, saying there was no way I wouldn't like *Eat a Peach*. I didn't like it, but she still put it on every time we were driving somewhere. I wanted to go to my room and review my materials for the next geography bee, but I didn't want to stop and talk and be asked questions about where I'd been all day. I was about to go back out the front door and sneak around to the kitchen patio, where I could slip inside without being seen, when I heard a noise coming from the upstairs apartments.

It was faint. A quiet jangling, like someone moving a teacup around a saucer by pushing it just lightly with the tip of their finger, bit by bit. It stopped for a moment, then started up again. It sounded cautious, almost secretive. I followed it up the stairs, moving very quietly and skipping the creaky steps. The lights were off and I kept my hand on the banister, thinking I would just take a peek over the top to satisfy my curiosity before going to my room, but when I got nearly all the way up I saw Elna in the shadows. She was crouched before one of the doorknobs, wedging something into the lock.

"Hey," I whispered.

She turned to me, startled, but quickly went back to what she was doing. Facing away, she said, "Don't you have keys to these rooms?"

"No," I told her. We had spares. Emergency keys. But they were on a ring on my mother's belt loop, always at her hip. I asked Elna what she was doing, now coming right up next to her, looking back and forth between her slim, pale hand jiggering what I could now see was a bobby pin and the steep, dark stairs. "What are you doing?" I repeated.

She paused and looked at me, then said simply, "I'm trying to get into Tom's room."

“You can’t do that,” I whispered, stunned and confused.

“Well, I am.”

“What if he comes back?”

“He won’t for another hour, don’t worry. I’ve been watching them since I got here and the truck always drops them off at the same time.”

“You can’t be sure of that. Sometimes there’s bad weather or an injury or something and they come back early.” I noticed a dryness creeping up my throat. “I was just outside and there was some rain.” My voice sounded limp. I could tell she didn’t care what I was saying. “What do you want to get in his room for?” I asked.

“I think he has something I could use,” she said. Her eyes were steely and trained on the lock. She had a little flashlight wedged between her cheek and shoulder. I recognized it from the junk drawer in our kitchen and wondered when she’d found it in there. Before I could say anything else, I heard the click of turning metal. Elna leaned back on her heels, a satisfied smirk on her face, and tucked the flashlight into her purse. She opened the door quietly, keeping her body pressed to the wall while she peeked around the bend, checking for any movement. Then, she slipped inside, leaving me alone in the hall. I didn’t want to go in there. I didn’t want to stay out, either. My chest was tight. There was a heaviness in my arms, like I’d been dragging around something twice my size. I didn’t know what else to do, so I followed her in.

Elna had the flashlight back out, and was flitting around the dim room, rifling through drawers and feeling around inside the grooves between the cushions on his futon. She went over to the kitchenette and opened each cabinet, running her hands over all the shelves, lifting up cans of soup and coffee. She stood on her toes and reached around the top of the fridge, holding the flashlight between her teeth. The whole apartment smelled stale. Like an old piece of bread that had been left sitting in a hot car. Dust bunnies collected in the corners. A big towel had been put up over the window, nailed directly into the wall by its corners. I noticed a homemade-looking blanket thrown across the top of the futon. Crocheted squares of many different colors. I could see what looked like burn holes from cigarettes along the edges. I thought someone must have made this blanket for Tom. His mother or grandmother, maybe. They probably gave it to him a long time ago. He'd probably been bringing it with him from place to place for years. Maybe he'd been sleeping with it since he was a child. The whole idea made me incredibly sad. I moved to straighten the blanket out and lay it smoothly across the futon, but stopped myself. I knew I shouldn't have been in there at all. I couldn't shift anything out of place. Elna, too, I noticed, was being careful to put everything back how she'd found it. She moved quietly and efficiently. Watching her, I got the idea that she'd done something like this before.

She left the kitchenette and disappeared into the bathroom. I could hear her rummaging. I was so uncomfortable I thought about just leaving without a word, but I found it impossible to move from where I stood. My whole body felt tense and frozen, tethered to the spot by its own nervousness.

A moment later, Elna emerged with a triumphant grin on her

face. She came right up to me and opened her purse. Inside, I saw a handful of baggies and orange plastic bottles. "See?" she said. "Told you he was on these." She picked one of the bottles up and held it to the flashlight. Little white ovals, no bigger than a watermelon seed, rolled around the bottom.

"Fine," I said, my voice hushed. "You were right. Put them back and let's go."

"I'm not putting them back, are you crazy?"

"What, you're just going to take them?"

"Yes," Elna hissed. "Do you understand how much I can sell these for when I get home? Of course I'm taking them. He'll just get more, anyway. Trust me." She gave me a quick pat on the shoulder, running her hand down my sleeve and rolling her eyes.

"Maybe he'll still pay you for the pants," I offered in a choked voice. It felt like a big stone had settled at the base of my throat.

"This isn't about five fucking dollars for a pair of pants." Elna shook her head. "Don't you get that?" She stood next to me, holding the purse up to my face again. "This is like, first and last on an apartment for me in LA. Maybe even a car."

"He'll notice they're gone right away," I said. I didn't understand what she meant by *first and last,* but I knew this wasn't the moment to ask about it.

"Yeah, but he won't think it was us. He'll think it was one of the other guys, or some woman he's had up here, for sure."

"Us," I repeated.

"Yeah." She smiled.

"I didn't steal anything."

"You're here in his room with me, aren't you?"

I couldn't come up with any words, so I just looked at the floor. She gave me a little squeeze around the waist and cocked her head to the side, pressing against me. Her hair fell down around my shoulder. Pieces of it caught in my eyelashes and the corner of my mouth. It smelled like smoke and candy. "Don't worry," she whispered. "Now, use that freaky memory of yours to give a good look around and make sure everything is where we found it." She gave a little knock to the back of my head.

"Everything's fine," I said. "Let's just go now." I pulled her by the wrist, nearly sick to my stomach.

"I should've checked under the bathroom sink," Elna muttered, glancing back behind her shoulder into the apartment. When we turned toward the door to leave, there was Tom.

The three of us stared at one another for a moment. Everything slowed down. Even the air became heavy. If I moved, I thought, it would be like wading through mud. Through the corner of my eye, I could see the color drop out of Elna's skin. She shifted on her feet and then took a step forward, as if to leave. Tom shook his head. He shut the door behind him, quietly, and walked into the room.

"What's all this?" he said. His voice was quiet, too. The stone in my throat turned to ice.

"We were just checking to see if your gas line was working," Elna said. Her lips spread into a big smile. "There were some issues in the building today."

"Yeah?"

"Yeah. There's no problem, so we were just going."

His gaze leveled at her purse, still unzipped, hanging half open at her side. A flash of recognition came into his eyes. He lunged forward with his good leg first, crossing half the room in just two wide steps, and yanked the bag from her arm. He tore through it, grabbing at the bottles and baggies inside. Now, his eyes were wild. Two shining black holes. He held the pills in his fists, then threw them down on the futon. He turned the bag upside down. All her things fell out: makeup, matches, dollar bills, a tomato pincushion stuck full of needles.

Elna fell to her knees and gathered her things. "You can't just grab my bag off me," she shrieked. He towered over her, hands curled into fists. I realized then how big he really was. The top of his head reached about six inches under the ceiling fan. His knuckles were bruised and purple. I could see a single vein, about as thick as a pencil, throbbing along the side of his neck.

"Why the fuck would you come in here and pull this type of shit?" he asked, his voice worryingly quiet. His chest was heaving. I could hear the wetness of his breaths. A damp rattling coming from deep within his throat.

"I wasn't pulling anything," Elna growled, getting up on her feet. She held her bag close to her chest.

"No? All this just happen to fall in your purse while you were checking the gas?" He gestured to the futon.

"Fine," Elna said. "Fine. We're just gonna get out of here. You have all your stuff, we're just going to leave."

Tom looked at me then, like he was just noticing I was in the apartment for the first time. I shrank against the wall, shoving my hands in my pockets to keep them from shaking. Down deep in the left one, my fingers brushed up against something unfamiliar.

Smooth plastic. A ridged cap. For a moment, I was bewildered. I couldn't understand how the bottle got in there. Everything that was happening felt unreal. A strange and fitful fever dream. But then my thoughts shuffled back to Elna, the way she'd leaned up against me minutes earlier, her hand running down the length of my jacket with its open pockets.

She walked past him quickly, bag still clutched to her chest. He watched, still as a log, unspeaking. I was terrified the bottle in my pocket would rattle, and he would notice it, and lunge at me like he had Elna. I wrapped my hand around it, trying to muffle any noise, and took a backward step toward the door. As Elna approached me, I saw her eyes dart down toward my pocket and then up at my face.

Tom said, "Don't let me find you in here again."

"You won't," Elna replied, rolling her eyes. A moment later, I heard her mutter *asshole* under her breath. And then, he sprung toward her, stumbling for a quick second before catching himself and hooking his arm around her neck, holding her in a tight choke. She grasped at him, and I could see she was trying to claw her nails into his skin. I could see her elbow gouging toward his gut in a series of frantic, useless shoves. And I could see that for the first time she looked really scared. The whites of her eyes appeared larger. Her skin, paler. Her lips were almost gray. Tom leaned toward her ear. His free hand crept up her chest, groping slowly around her bra line and then over her left breast. He brushed her hair aside with his chin. A sick, sour feeling shot through me when he did that. It started in my gut and moved down into the tips of my fingers in an instant.

I heard him say, "What was that?" Elna's mouth moved, but no sound came out. He squeezed tighter, pressing his lips even closer to her ear, "You made a big mistake coming in here, you skanky little bitch." He gave a long look at the side of her face, then at me, then at nothing. His expression was strange, still on the surface but I could sense the rage churning. It seemed like he was thinking about something, though I couldn't tell exactly what.

Then, without warning, he let go of Elna. She fell to the ground, then scrambled to her feet and we both ran, hand in hand, down the stairs and out the door into the cold air.

12

When I woke up in the morning, I heard the voices of men in the store. I lay there still, just listening, trying to understand what they were saying. I was sure they were looking for me and my cousin, that there was a whole mob of them spreading the story of what happened the day before. A film of cold sweat gathered on my palms. I tried to think about what I could say, how I could explain it, but nothing came to me. I listened harder. I shut my eyes and focused on the tangle of their voices all together, separating each one out like a ball of knotted thread, my palms growing clammier. I heard the words *Wednesday, overtime, Christmas Eve.* I realized they weren't talking about my cousin and me at all. They were talking about shift assignments. Someone offered a Slim Jim to someone else. There was light laughter. The door opening and shutting. The sound of a truck idling.

After they'd left, I went and sat at the counter, already fifteen minutes later than I should've opened the register. All I could think about was Elna, wondering when she would come out and what she'd say. The bottle of pills was still in the pocket of my jacket, hanging on the back of my bedroom door. I wanted her to tell me what to do with it, for her to take it back so that I wouldn't have to think about it anymore. Yesterday, after running out of the house, we walked in silence, arms linked, looping the town's main street. A couple times, I opened my mouth to say something, wanting some reassurance from her, wanting to hear her tell me that she was okay and that I was okay and that somehow what just happened wasn't as big a deal as it felt like, but every time I turned to her to speak she threw me a sharp look, warning the words from leaving my lips. So we went on quietly, coming back home when the streetlights flicked on, each going to our rooms without a word.

Around ten, a woman came in and bought a box of baking soda. Thirty minutes later, she came back for flour and cigarettes. I replaced the roll of receipt paper in the till. I straightened up the magazines. Hours passed and Elna didn't emerge from her room. I so badly wanted her to put makeup on me, like she'd been doing, and for everything to be the way it was before we went into Tom's apartment. I wished I could undo every moment of it, to scrub it from time completely. After a while, my mother came in to sign for a beer delivery and took over the counter. I walked down to Elna's door and just stood there, listening, my hand poised to knock, but instead I went to my own room and put the makeup on myself.

I only had a few things. A lip gloss she'd given me earlier in the week. Cherry flavor. A clumpy old tube of mascara from the brief time we sold it in the store. A jar of body glitter someone had dropped in one of the parking spaces out front. It had the consistency of thick jam and was flaked with chunky, iridescent sparkles. It was advertised heavily in all the magazines. I saw it smeared on the cheeks and collarbones of all the cool girls at school. Elna had several different ones. Lavender, pale pink, pearl white. I'd urged my mother to buy me a bottle of it when we were at the drugstore once. She held the bottle in her hand and looked at it with suspicion, then at me, then placed it back on the shelf. "You're fourteen," she said flatly. "And this is for strippers." The one I'd found on the ground was silver like a fresh coin. I dabbed it over my eyelids and then blinked at myself in the mirror.

Jen brought a pizza over for lunch later in the afternoon. The three of us sat around the table together, eating off grease-soaked paper plates. My mother kept looking at my face, frowning at the glitter on my eyes. I pretended I didn't notice. Finally, she asked, "Where's your cousin?"

"Sleeping in, I guess."

"The day's halfway done."

"Maybe she's not feeling well," I said.

"She has to eat something."

"The human body can survive up to three months without food," I said.

My mother shot me a glare. Jen cleared her throat, looking between us, then added, "I'm sure she'll come out when she feels like it."

"The pizza will be cold." My mother lifted the lid of the box, peeking inside. Orangey circles of pepperoni stuck to the top of the cardboard.

"She's probably feeling down about the holidays," Jen said quietly.

"You think so?"

"I would be," Jen said with a shrug. "To be all the way up here, no idea what's going on at home. Sure, you're family, but she doesn't know you all that well."

"Candace still hasn't called," my mother whispered, glancing down the hall toward Elna's door. She crossed her arms, then cast a gloomy look over her shoulder toward the telephone. "I left a message at the facility the other day. Nothing."

"Maybe tomorrow? Christmas Eve."

"Maybe," my mother said. She shook her head. There was a glazed look in her eyes. She finished her slice and then added, "What do you think they do in there for Christmas?"

"In the rehab?" Jen put her glass down. "I'm sure they do something nice."

"I don't think it's nice," my mother clipped. "I'm just imagining her in there with a pair of those socks on. The ones with the rubber on the bottoms? Eating some kind of canned slop off a plastic tray." She crossed her arms and sat back in the chair. Her voice cracked a little when she said *tray.*

Jen glanced at me with widened eyes, then back at my mother. "Listen, I'll cut down a little pine tree from my yard," she said. "I'll bring it over here for dinner. I'll bring lights, too. That'll be nice." I could tell she was trying to change the subject.

It occurred to me then that my mother might be sad about the state of her sister's life. I'd never had a thought like that before. Candace existed in such a distant orbit from our little world, dropping in only once every so often to talk for hours on the phone, or to make an extraordinarily rare appearance in her dented-up car. I hadn't wondered much about their life together as girls, what it was like to grow up in Idaho or whether they were close when they were young. I knew they both moved away from their hometown the same year. Candace at eighteen to California to try and become famous, somehow. My mother when she was twenty to Seattle, where she managed a school cafeteria for a while, and then to Mineral after she'd heard through a friend of a friend about a small business for sale in a mountain town, housing included. I knew they had a younger brother who died as an infant. I knew that Candace had won a county pageant and was crowned Miss Kootenai Potato Princess during her senior year of high school, and that my mother sewed her gown, even making a sash with little sateen potatoes all along it. She'd stuffed them with pillow filling, to make them puffy and stand out in pictures. My mother still had a photo of Candace in it, wearing her tiara and standing next to a record-setting, twenty-pound russet potato, which she told me about when she was loopy and feverish with the flu. The next week, when she was better, I asked to see the photo and she kept telling me she'd find it later. I asked again and again. Finally, she told me it had gotten lost.

I don't know why I felt like I needed to ask about it again then, with Jen at the table, after years of not bringing it up at all or even really thinking about it. But I found myself saying, "Did you ever find the potato picture?"

"What?" my mother said, her voice thin.

"The picture of Aunt Candace in her gown, with the huge potato."

"Oh." She frowned. "No. I haven't seen that photo in a long time."

"What's that about?" Jen asked. Her mouth was full of pizza. She wiped her face with the sleeve of her fleece jacket.

"Nothing, it was just this ridiculous thing in the seventies." My mother got up and started to straighten things out on the counter. It wasn't even a mess. Nothing needed fixing. Still, she shuffled around the kitchen, tidying for a few minutes before coming back to the table and pointing a finger, one eyebrow raised. "I want you to be more careful making change at the register, by the way," she said.

"I am careful."

"Oh?"

"Yeah," I told her. "I'm a very precise counter."

"Well, we were off by twenty when I cashed out yesterday."

I looked down at the table. My mouth felt a little dry, suddenly. I said, "Are you sure? Maybe *you* miscounted."

"No, I don't believe I did."

"We all make mistakes from time to time," Jen interjected. Her voice sounded the way it always did when she sensed an argument brewing between us. We all looked at one another.

"Well, let's all be more careful, then," my mother said, folding her napkin in her lap. "You tell your cousin to be careful, too," she added, one eyebrow still raised.

Later that day, after lunch, Jen came into my bedroom while I was sitting at my desk, going through my geography practice cards. Practice wasn't even the point. I knew them all by heart. I just wanted to feel the familiar weight of them in my hands, the way the laminate faces slid smoothly off one another. Silently, I mouthed the names of countries and capitals, official languages, and years of independence. Ten cards in, the low murmur of anxiety that seemed to always hover above me, like a cloud, began to clear. I didn't have to think about Tom. I could think about the facts printed on the cards. I could climb inside the filing cabinet in my head and stay there, where everything made perfect sense.

Jen knocked gently and then opened the door a crack. I was a little surprised. She didn't usually come in my room. "How's it going?" she asked.

"All right." I looked at her, still holding the card for Belize. "Why?"

"You seem a little stressed today."

"Everything's fine," I said.

"Everything?" She closed the door behind her and sat on the edge of the bed, facing me. I put the cards down and looked at her. "Nothing you want to talk to me about?"

"Why would you think there would be?" I asked.

"Big changes around here," she said. "Your cousin coming to stay and everything. That isn't such a small thing to adjust to."

"It isn't a huge thing to adjust to, either."

"Sure," Jen said, nodding. She looked around my room. I watched as her eyes moved from the stack of magazines to the flags in the pen cup, the closet, and the nightstand where the stolen mood ring still sat. Then, to the door, where my coat with the pill bottle hung. My heart fluttered. She smiled a little and said, "When I was your age, I had a plastic bubble aquarium in my room that was full of sea monkeys. I sent away for them from a comic book ad."

"Brine shrimp," I said.

"Is that what they are? I thought they were little baboons." I rolled my eyes. She chuckled, then cleared her throat. "Listen," she said, "is Elna being nice to you?"

"Nice?" I put the cards in my desk drawer and shut it. A queasy feeling started in my stomach and spread quickly through the rest of me. "Why would you ask me that?"

"Just checking. I know kids aren't always nice."

"Elna isn't like other kids."

"How so?"

"She's just . . ." I flapped my hands around, trying to come up with the right word. "I don't know, she's been surfing. She went to see Third Eye Blind."

"What is that, a band?"

"Yes." I sighed, though I hadn't even heard of them before Elna told me the story of going to the concert.

"I see."

"You don't like her," I said.

"I didn't say that."

"You don't have to say it," I replied. "I can tell that you don't."

"She's a child. What is she, sixteen? I don't like her or dislike her. That isn't even the point." Jen shook her head. "All I'm trying to say is, I think she's a different sort of kid than you."

"So?" I snapped.

"*So,* I know you're spending a lot of time with her, but I think maybe you should take it a little slow."

"Take what slow?"

"Just, you know, getting too close to her too quick."

"I'm not an idiot," I snapped.

"That is one thing I've never thought you were, Ida." Jen rubbed her eyebrows like there was pain inside her head.

"So then why are you acting like I can't tell for myself who's my friend or not?"

"Look." She let out a long breath. "I know you think she's the greatest thing."

"You don't know what I think about her."

"And I know a lot of girls your age find themselves wanting to be more like an older girl they look up to—"

"I don't want to be like her," I said.

"No?"

"No." I crossed my arms. "Maybe you don't know me as well as you thought."

Jen studied my face for a while. There was a sad sort of half smile on her mouth. "I know you sneak out sometimes," she said. Her voice wasn't accusatory, and it didn't have that tint of satisfaction some adults got when catching a teenager in some act of deceit. It was just plain. Almost like she didn't care, but not quite. I looked at her. "In the mornings. You slip back in with wet hair."

"When have you seen me doing that?" I asked, surprised.

"Once, last summer, I was walking home early and saw you climbing back in your window. Then again this September. The day after Labor Day, same thing."

"Oh," I said. I wondered if anyone else had seen me.

"I don't know what you do. I don't really want to know, because it isn't my business and I think a kid of your age is supposed to have secrets. But I am telling you that I want you to be safe and careful wherever you go, whoever you go with."

"All right," I told her.

Jen nodded and left my room, shutting the door softly behind her. I lay in my bed for a while, staring up at the ceiling. I pulled the collar of my sweatshirt up and rubbed the glitter off my eyes until the skin felt raw.

13

I woke up late the morning of Christmas Eve to my mother in the kitchen, toiling. Every bowl and whisk and knife we owned seemed to be out on the counter. The oven ticked and hissed, gearing itself up. I stood there, off to the side, blocked from the cabinet that held our breakfast cereals by a large butcher paper–wrapped package. I could smell the meat inside of it. Bloody metallic and a little sweet. My mother pulled a roasting pan out of a drawer, examined it, then put it back and went digging for something else. Perspiration shimmered on her ruddy, wide brow.

Before I could ask her anything, she said, "I'm doing a hundred things in here. Just go eat something from the shop when you get hungry." I stood there for a few moments longer, watching her slice open a plastic bag of onions. They tumbled across the counter. She gathered them into a pile. They rolled apart again.

Before Jen, she was pretty casual about holidays. Some Christmases, we'd just order lo mein and shrimp toast and eat straight out of the paper cartons at the small kitchen table, which I thought was great. Sometimes we'd watch *Miracle on 34th Street* on tape. But now, each year, she'd be up early, frazzled and determined with many magazine-torn recipes pushpinned to the cabinets. She'd clear the dining table that sat in the little room between the kitchen and the store, and put away the stacks of mail, folded clothes, and overflow stock that sat in the hallway nearly every other day. For Easter, she'd bought a special cake pan in the shape of a lamb. It lived in the pantry, where it sat with its blank, steely expression on the top shelf, untouched, until the one day a year it was pressed into service. The whole thing was kind of a production—removing the cake from the pan in one piece, decorating it with a fluffy coconut frosting, and giving it eyes, and a little nose, and the curve of a mouth. She even dyed the leftover coconut shreds with green food coloring to give it a bed of grass to lie down in upon the platter.

I walked down the hallway and into the store. It was colder than the kitchen, and the floor was full of morning creaks. I took a package of Yodels from the shelf and sat at the register, eating them while I shuffled through my practice cards. The next bee was in July, in Tacoma at a Marriott on Commerce Street. Ballroom C. I'd read the invitation many times, already. We were to arrive no later than eight in the morning, and the bee would begin at nine. There were three judges. Judy and John Fisher, who were both social studies teachers in Seattle. A man named Otis Moore, who'd written a book on cartography and looked to be about a hundred years old. Their glowering faces were printed in black and white, along with a list of recommended preparatory materials and driving directions. There would be thirty other contestants. Almost all boys, as usual. It bothered me a lot when we were just waiting around backstage, and I'd have to stand there with them while they all pretended to fight one another, leaping on each other's shoulders and throwing weak punches, taking a pause every so often to stare at me and the one or two other girls. But once we got on stage and the questions started, I couldn't really hear or see or think about anything else.

After about an hour, Elna emerged from her room. She marched right over to the counter and picked up the phone. I looked at her for signs of yesterday, but found nothing. She had on an outfit that reminded me of something the main character of a movie would wear on the first day of school. She didn't look at me, or say anything. Just lifted the phone to her ear and dialed a number that was written on her wrist in black Sharpie.

"What are you doing?" I whispered.

"I'm calling my mother."

"I thought you didn't know the number."

"It wasn't hard to find." She nodded toward the kitchen. She must have come out of her room last night and got it from the mess of notes and papers around our personal telephone.

I felt like I shouldn't be right there while she was on this particular call, so I got up and walked slowly through the rows of shelves, trying to occupy myself. The shop was always closed on the 24th and 25th of December, the curtain drawn over the door window. Always the same little sign in my mother's careful cursive, reading *Merry Christmas!*

By the entrance, there were things like sunflower seeds and peanuts and jerky in bags. Then, sundries. Flour, sugar, salt, baking powder. One single, mysterious container of cream of tartar, which had been there for so long it was as if it had sprouted from the shelf spontaneously, like a mushroom, and been allowed to stay, rooted in place. I could hear Elna saying the name *Candace Robinson* into the phone. Her voice was measured, but irritated. It sounded like she was trying to keep quiet. I suspected she didn't want my mother to get involved. I rounded the bend into the next aisle. We had flimsy plastic fly swatters in five colors. I paused to rearrange them in order. *I am family,* I heard Elna say. *I'm her daughter.* I straightened out a few bags of briquettes. I noticed there were no Band-Aids left, so I went to the store closet in the corner where we kept extra of everything, and put a few more boxes on the shelf. *No,* she hissed. *I can't try again later.* I ran my fingers over the covers of a stack of black-and-white composition notebooks. Next to these were yellow pencils, paper clips packaged into bundles of twenty-five, felt-tip pens with red, blue, black ink.

From the kitchen, I heard my mother let out a quick shriek, then the sound of the faucet. I was sure she'd burned herself touching a hot pan without a towel. She did that every year. I went back over near the register, to the cold-case, and got a Snapple. Elna's posture slumped farther and farther down as she listened to the voice on the other end. She rubbed at her brow, smudging some of her dark eyeliner out over her temple. A few moments later, she said, "All right, thanks." After hanging up the phone, she just stood there, blank-faced.

"What happened?" I asked.

"She's getting switched to an outpatient program, apparently."

"What does that mean?"

"It basically means she gets to go home now."

"But I thought the court said—"

"I know," Elna cut me off. "But they're running out of beds, or something. She's halfway through her program, so the judge had her sign something saying she'll go every day to a place near home to finish."

"To do what, exactly?"

"Just the regular stuff," Elna snapped. "Meetings and piss tests and whatever." We heard the tinny clatter of an aluminum pot hitting the floor and rolling. "What the hell is going on in there?" she asked.

"A prime rib, I think."

"Fancy," Elna said.

"It's only because Jen's coming over."

"I don't care if it's because the pope is coming. I'm starving. I didn't really eat yesterday."

I reached into the back of the case and pulled out a ham and cheese Lunchables. Elna held it in her hands, inspecting it for a moment, then sat down on the floor opposite me and tore it open. "Were you okay?" I asked.

"I don't know," she said, shrugging. "I guess."

"You didn't come out of your room all day."

"Have you seen him?" She put the whole stack of cheese slices in her mouth at once.

"I think I heard him yesterday morning with the rest of the group but he hasn't come around or anything." She nodded, chewing.

I asked, "Do you think he will?" I was suddenly very nervous. She didn't answer for a while, which worried me more.

"I don't want to scare you, but I saw him outside my window last night," she finally said.

My chest went cold. "What do you mean?" I whispered.

"I mean, he was out there." She pointed toward the side of the house where her spare room was. "At like, ten at night maybe. I got up to go to the bathroom and get some water, and when I came back and shut the light off I saw him standing there."

I pictured the space between our shop and the building next door. When I was little, it had been a game processor. I could remember the smell of guts cut with fresh blood drifting through our open windows in the summer. Then it became a Maytag appliance dealer. Now, it sat empty. There'd been a *For lease* sign stuck in the ground out front for three years.

"Was he looking in at you?" I asked. My tongue felt huge and dry, like a big slab of cardboard shoved into my mouth.

"He was smoking. Just leaning on the side of the building. I crouched down, trying to get an idea of what he was up to. I started to think he couldn't see me, like maybe he didn't even know he was facing into my room."

"Then what?" I asked. I pressed my nails into my palms, hard, trying to calm my mounting anxiety.

"When I finally stood up to close the curtain, he smiled right at me and winked." I sat there as she finished eating, watching her peel the ham apart and puncture the silver pouch of juice with the little attached straw. She offered me a sip and I shook my head no. My whole mouth felt dry, but I was too unsettled to want to drink anything. Every nerve in my body was raw and fragile. Just the thought of the artificial fruit flavor hitting my tongue, the jolt of sugar and fake orange, made me want to gag. So I just stayed still, looking down at the purplish red half-moons indented deep into the flesh of my palms.

14

Later in the day, my mother corralled Elna and me into the kitchen to help her with dinner. "Time for you two to make yourselves useful," she commanded, pushing a bag of potatoes across the table toward us. It skidded to a stop just in front of my elbows. I could smell the dirt and loam. "Peel those," she said, dropping two paring knives down before us. "Then cut them into quarters."

We sat there quietly, the potatoes slipping under our fingers as we removed their skins. A heavy weight seemed to hang on Elna now. Her shoulders were slumped low, her mouth set in a tense, thin line. She looked almost gray in the face. Even her handling of the potatoes was clumsy, nothing like her sewing. She dropped a half-finished one into her lap and just stared down at it, blank in the eyes, before picking it up and slamming it back down on the table.

I looked out the window over to the Arthurs' house. Frost gathered on their shingles. Patrick's car was still parked in the same spot. I could see a mess of CDs, uncovered, splayed out across the dashboard. Prisms refracted off their silver sides, casting little strips of rainbow light around the inside of the car. I wondered if he'd managed to catch the snake. I wondered how long he would stay around Mineral, and if you could rejoin the military after they'd kicked you out. My guess was no, you couldn't. I wondered why they kicked him out in the first place. I wondered why he didn't go with any of the logging operations. In just a couple months, their season would be over, and a lot of the workers would leave. Our rooms upstairs would clear out. A handful of new people, usually not associated with the lumber companies, would come through. Thinking about it took the edge off my worry a little bit. Just to remember that soon Tom would be gone, somebody else in his place. Sometimes we got renters from the U.S. Forest Service, posted on a surveying assignment for a month or two. Sometimes hikers taking a break from the Pacific Crest Trail. My mother loved the hikers. They always did mountains of laundry and bought us out of snacks and toilet paper.

My favorite boarder we'd ever had was in one of the offseasons. She only stayed a month. A young woman named Felicity who'd been given a grant from Washington State University to study slugs in the area. Banana slugs, black slugs, leopard slugs. Mineral had tons of them.

"Are you an entomologist?" I asked on her first day in. She was rooting around in the trunk of her car, gathering up the contents of a bag of notebooks and pens that had spilled open on the drive. I'd been standing off to the side in the store, listening, when she'd arrived just twenty minutes earlier and paid my mother and introduced herself.

"No, a *malacologist,*" she told me. "Slugs are actually mollusks. They're more closely related to octopuses than they are to insects." I liked this woman immediately, and stood there just watching her for a minute. She turned to me again, hand on her hip, and said, "Did you know octopuses' brains are ring-shaped?"

"No," I replied. "I didn't know that."

"They're wrapped around their esophagi, like a donut. That's why octopuses need to take very small bites and chew their food carefully with their beak until it's totally pulverized. Because if they take too big a bite, it will press along the sides of their throat and damage their delicate brain."

"That's interesting," I said. I leaned on the side of her car, arms crossed, looking at the ground, thinking about it.

"Yes, it is. You may also be interested to know they actually have nine brains. The main one I just told you about, and then eight small ones at the base of each of their tentacles."

"How do you know so much about octopuses?" I asked.

"When I was in undergrad, I went down to California to study them. Giant Pacific ones in Half Moon Bay." She slung her bag over her shoulder and grinned at me. "Anyway," she said. "I'm getting paid for slugs at the moment. Can you point me toward the forest?"

I directed her toward the trail up to Needle Lake, where I knew lived an abundance of slugs. She went there every day.

Sometimes our paths would cross while I was returning from school and she was returning from the woods. I was always happy to see her coming up the other end of the road with her khaki overalls, specimen jar in hand. She loved soft, creeping things the way I loved maps, and here she was on her own, spending all her time singularly focused on them, alone in the woods every day. I was nine then. I'd never really met an adult that I wanted to be like before. And I think she must have realized that, because she'd take time to sit down on the porch with me and show me whatever new creature was inside the jar, patiently explaining all the parts of her research.

After she left, my mother said, "Bright girl. A bit touched, though."

"What do you mean?" I asked.

"Talked my ear off this morning about some type of snail she found underneath the porch. She told me they would multiply quickly, and if I ever wanted to get rid of them not to use poison, but to fill a water bottle with chopped garlic and coffee grounds and to splash it all around. Asked me at least three times if I had fresh garlic."

"I liked her," I said.

"I noticed," my mother replied.

Thinking about Felicity brought a warm feeling to my chest. I wondered what she was doing, five years later. Maybe the university was still sending her off to different places to fill up her notebooks and jars. She'd once mentioned to me being interested in sea slugs. *Nudibranchs,* they were called. The tide pools on the Olympic coast were full of them. As I peeled the potatoes, I imagined her there, crouching over the swirling salt water in her overalls.

Suddenly, Elna shrieked in pain, jerking up out of her chair, holding her hand out before her. Blood gushed from the webbing between her thumb and forefinger, splattering the cut potatoes. I watched, stunned, as she dashed to the sink, knocking over an opened bag of Domino on the way. A waterfall of sugar fell from the counter to the floor. She held her hand under the faucet, face fixed in a grimace. The blood splotches on the potatoes started to turn dark around the edges. My mother watched all of this, then marched over to the table and gathered up all the quartered potatoes in a bowl. She nudged Elna out of the way by the sink, and rinsed off each potato piece by piece.

"Are we still going to eat those?" I asked, feeling a little sick.

"Yes," she said. "They're fine." Elna looked grayer in the face now. She was holding her injured hand limply before her chest, like a wounded kitten. I could see my mother roll her eyes as she set the bowl down on the counter. She tossed a dishrag to my cousin and said, "You're all right, aren't you? That can't be too deep." I retrieved a dustpan from the cabinet and began to sweep up the sugar, kneeling on the floor. A cold draft wafted in from the porch door. The hair on my arms stood up. When I went to toss the dirty sugar in the trash, Elna and I bumped into each other, and the sugar spilled all over the ground again.

"You know what," my mother said, throwing her hands up. "Probably best for you two to get out of my hair for a while."

"Won't you need help?" I asked.

"You can help with the dishes later." She took the dustpan forcefully from my grip, and shooed us out into the hallway.

Even in the dim light, I could see how queasy Elna looked. "Are you all right?" I asked.

She steadied herself against the wall, cradling her hand carefully against her middle. "I think I just need some fresh air," she said.

No cars were out on the road. Colored lights twinkled on a few of the streetlamps. A wet chill hung all around us. Flurries of snow fell from the clouds, a thin layer gathering on the ground. I could smell smoke drifting from nearby chimneys. Beneath it, the smell of the cold itself—crisp and clean and slightly sweet. I felt responsible for my cousin, somehow. Like it was up to me to entertain her now that we'd been banished from the kitchen. I stood there with my hands in my pockets, thinking about where to go. I didn't want to bring her toward town, where I knew people would be shopping the night before Christmas.

"What are we supposed to do now?" Elna asked. I'd gotten her a Band-Aid, which she'd wrapped carefully around her cut before putting on a pair of winter gloves. We were both bundled in our coats and boots, standing together on the sidewalk.

"I could show you Needle Lake, I guess."

"Where you sneak out to go swimming?"

"Yeah," I said with a nod.

"Isn't it up on some hill?"

"That way," I said, pointing toward the old lumber road.

"How far is it?"

"It's closer than it looks."

"Whatever," Elna said. "Let's just walk."

She was quiet as we made our way down the muddy path. I kept looking at the side of her face, trying to figure out what was happening inside her head. It was strange to walk there with another person. I'd only ever gone alone. We passed by the spot where I'd once drifted asleep, and another where I'd found a fallen bird's nest, still full of peeping, featherless chicks. I pointed to a large rock off on the side and said, "That's an erratic boulder." Elna looked at it, then back at the horizon. "It tumbled off a glacier millions of years ago. When it first landed here, this area was covered in four hundred feet of ice." As we continued on, I tried to think of other things to say, but nothing seemed right. I wished I was alone and could just keep going until dusk, not having to worry about another person.

When I saw the familiar clearing in the trees and the first part of the trail peeking out from a tangle of rocks and roots, I stopped and waved her over. "That's the way up," I said. Elna looked ahead, arms crossed over her stomach. We stood at the opening, our breath forming little clouds. Moss hung in thick ropes from the branches, green and shimmering with dew. "There's no snow in there," Elna said, squinting into the dim canopy of trees.

"That's because the trail crosses two ecosystems," I told her, relieved to have something I could explain. "This part is actually a montane rainforest, so it's a lot warmer in there than out here in the open air. It's really humid, even in winter."

"So you're saying it won't be cold up there?"

"Not for a while. We'll probably be too warm in our coats, even. But then partway there we'll cross into the subalpine zone, and there'll be snow."

"A lot of it?"

"Some," I said. "We won't know how much until we get up there." I glanced down at our boots. They were fine enough, but if I'd known we were going all the way up the trail I would've worn thicker socks. Elna crouched down and tightened her laces. "How far is the actual lake from here?" she asked.

"Maybe thirty minutes, if we don't take any breaks."

"And is it part of the rainforest or what?"

"It's in the alpine zone," I said.

"Crazy," she muttered, standing up and dusting off her jacket.

"Washington has a really unique biome."

"Well, sure," Elna replied. "It's what brought me here. I just had to experience the biome for myself." She set off then onto the trail, and I followed behind.

It was much quieter inside the forest than out on the mud road. No birds chirped, and any sounds of nearby eighteen-wheelers were muted out by the dense rows of ancient, craggy trunks. Loggers weren't allowed to cut in here. This whole swath of woods was off-limits. On the other side of the mountain, past the lake, there was a newly licensed timber field. I'd never gone out that way. Some of our boarders were taking contracts there, I knew. But this side was protected under an old federal law. There'd been a plaque about it a long time ago, just a small piece of enameled metal screwed into one of the trees with a paragraph about the local man who'd fought to save this half of the mountain a century earlier. When I was small, it was already partially covered by encroaching bark. Now, you couldn't see it at all.

The light grew dimmer as we moved farther along, blotted out by the broad cover of leaves and hanging moss all thatched together many feet above our heads. Our footsteps were silent over the thick layers of fallen pine needles. The only sound I could hear was the soft jingle of Elna's charm bracelet. Diving underwater quieted my brain and made me feel free from the world, even just for a little while, but walking here in the rainforest made me feel that I was protected, somehow. Like the trees really were alive in the way that a person is alive, and that they noticed me at their feet and wanted me to be safe from danger. When I was alone, I took the time to touch them as I went. Just pressing my hand against their trunks for a few moments to let them know I could hear their thoughts. But it wasn't something I wanted Elna to see, so I just kept walking alongside her, hands in my pockets.

After a while, we stopped to sit on the trunk of a huge fallen red cedar that ran diagonally over the path. Elna unzipped her jacket and stuffed her gloves down into a pocket. "It really is warm in here," she said. Her face looked a little better to me now, less gray and sunken. I looked at the bandage between her two fingers. A dark blot of dried blood showed through the gauze.

"Does your cut still hurt?" I asked.

"Not too much."

"Are you sad about your mom getting moved out of the hospital?"

"Doesn't make a difference to me where she is," she replied.

I didn't believe her, but I also didn't feel like I should press it any further, so instead, I asked, "Are you worried about Tom?" She shrugged in response. "What did you do after you saw him looking in at you?" I pressed.

"What do you think? Closed the blinds and made sure my door was locked." I crossed my arms over my stomach, feeling uneasy, as I imagined him smiling in the dark. "I've thought he was kind of a creep since I got here, I guess," she added.

"What do you mean?"

"He just stares a lot, and shoots me gross looks sometimes if I walk by."

"I didn't know," I said. "Besides the other night I've only really seen him down in the laundry room with you."

"I had sort of a weird feeling about him already by then but what was I going to do? Not take his money? He'd never actually done anything, and I told you I really need to be saving up right now."

A yellow banana slug crept across a nearby patch of moss. "Anyway, here," she added, digging around in one of her coat pockets. "I got this for you when I went back to the store for more sewing needles." She opened her palm to reveal a key chain with a see-through plastic globe, about the size of a Ping-Pong ball, full of half-blue liquid and half-clear. In the center, where the two colors met, was a tiny figurine of a girl in an orange swimsuit with her arms outstretched in a diving position. "Merry Christmas. Shake it around," Elna said. I did. The blue and clear mixed together, bubbling and separating like salad dressing. The girl twirled around violently, always ending up back in the middle, arms upward. "It made me think of you." I shook the key chain again, watching the little storm inside. I looped it through the zipper pull on my parka.

"I didn't get you anything," I told her.

"That's okay," she said, hopping off the trunk.

As we approached the last section of forest, the ground grew drier and steeper. We stepped over crooked rocks, using low-hanging branches to guide ourselves across a small stream. The muscles in my thighs burned.

"Isn't this bad for your heart?" Elna asked.

"It's fine," I said. "I've done it a bunch of times." Really, it was exactly the kind of thing I wasn't supposed to do. It was two miles up, with one area where you had to crawl over large, exposed tree roots and a section where you needed to grab a rope tied around a tree trunk to hoist yourself up a ledge.

Only once did this hike cause me any trouble. Last summer, when I was sneaking up to the lake early one morning. It happened around the halfway point. I could feel my heart getting overwhelmed, a tense pressure building in my chest. I leaned my back against a tree. For a moment, my vision blurred and blacked out around the edges, leaving only a pinhole of light and color at the center. For some reason, I'd had a nagging worry that if I passed out and hit my head and died I would never be able to dig up the time capsule I'd buried in the yard. It contained a selection of my favorite things and a letter I'd written to myself, to be opened in the year 2017. But I didn't faint, and so I kept going back, letting Dr. Fields' warnings fade into static as I climbed higher up the mountain.

Soon we emerged from the wooded area into the open side of the ridge, where the trail wound around a steady stream of glacial runoff and continued upward about a quarter mile before ending at the lake. "A lot of snow," Elna said. "People really come up here in the winter?"

"Yeah," I replied, pressing my foot down into it to see how far up my leg it reached. Only a little past my ankle, but up in the distance I could see drifts that settled high against trees. "Are you cold?" I asked.

"I'm okay." She zipped her coat all the way up to her chin and pulled her gloves back on. I looked up at the sky. There were probably a couple hours of sunlight left. If we got to the lake soon, we could hang out for a while and still manage to get back before dusk settled. I'd actually only come up here in winter once before, though I didn't mention that to Elna. I knew that if the temperature dropped low enough, someone from the town would rope off an area for skating. I didn't own skates, of course. I wouldn't have been allowed to learn how to use them. But I did hike up last January one early morning. I'd had a bad argument with my mother before bed and lay awake all night, stewing. The silent walk cleared my thoughts, as it always did, and when I got to the top of the mountain I just stood alone on the ice for a while, content to look out at the frosted trees along the shore before anyone else had woken up. It hadn't gotten cold enough yet for skating this year, I didn't think. Usually they put a sign up at the intersection. I imagined Elna knew how to skate. Or, if she didn't, she would pick it up right away, fooling everyone into thinking she'd been doing it for a long time.

We floundered along together over the stream, clutching each other's hands for balance as we stepped carefully across slick rocks. As we trudged, a red fox darted across our path. Our gazes connected and the three of us paused for a moment, frozen in awe of one another.

By the time we reached the lake, Elna's cheeks were bright with cold. She seemed more relaxed now, even smiling a little as we came upon the shoreline. The world around us was still and white. Void of foot tracks, utterly quiet. I followed her down the embankment and toward the dock. She navigated the final stretch far ahead of me, lifting her long legs through the snow one at a time in a strangely graceful march before leaping over a pile of stones from an abandoned firepit. There was an open wine bottle discarded in the center, its neck sticking out from layers of sleet. Frost creeping up the glass. I knew people came up here to drink and lose their virginity during the summer. I overheard things about it in the bathroom at school. If Elna lived in Mineral, she would be one of the girls whose conversations I'd eavesdrop on from a closed stall, my feet tucked up on the toilet seat. I stood on top of a rock and looked out at the lake. Snow had gathered in a low drift along one side of the water. The rest was a shining, black slick of ice stretching all the way to the other shore.

Elna looked back at me from the edge of the dock, about fifteen feet out onto the lake, hand on her hip. I felt a little twinge in my chest as I climbed up the final stretch to meet her, pushing my heart to work even harder. Fog hung low in the air, hovering just below the tree line. Jagged pine tops disappeared inside of it. We stood side by side, gazing out. A red cardinal flitted by. When the wind blew, swirls of loose snow fell from the drift and turned to mist in the air.

"I can see why you like it up here. It's pretty," she said. "Now I wish I'd come during the summer."

"You could come back," I offered.

"Maybe," she said. "After you come to California." She gave me a quick wink and a nudge on the side. I curled my toes inside my boots, peering over the ledge down onto the ice. Deep cracks cut through the reflection of my face. I thought about all the frogs and fish and snapping turtles, dormant in the cold mud. "I meant what I said about not being sad about my mom, by the way," Elna said, her voice suddenly tight.

"Why aren't you?"

"I can't do anything about it." She shrugged. "I can't make her different." She tucked her hair behind her ears. "Whenever I've tried to help her, she just lies and I end up finding out about it later. Like, a few years ago I went through this whole checklist with her every day that her caseworker gave me, and I walked her to meetings every night, and I'd even sit there in the meetings with her. They really sucked, too. They were like, super long and had the most disgusting coffee. And then it turned out the whole time she was keeping pills in the handle of her hairbrush. I only found out when I dropped it on the floor once and it broke open, and then she got mad at *me.*" My cousin let out a little scoff.

"Why would the caseworker give the checklist to you?" I asked.

"Why not me?"

"Well, you were only like, thirteen." Elna looked at me for a long time. I averted my eyes toward the lake's far shore, uncomfortable with holding her stare. Even when I wasn't looking, I could feel her on my skin. A faint prickle traveled up and down my cheek.

After a while she said, "I was actually twelve."

"Who helped her while you were at school?"

"No one, I guess. But I missed a lot of school then. It was the end of the year, anyway. It didn't really matter."

"Did you have a favorite class?" I asked. She let out a loud, sharp laugh. It echoed across the lake. I didn't understand what was funny.

A quiet moment passed, and then she said, "I guess I liked algebra." She bent down and gathered up a handful of snow, forming it into a ball between her palms. I watched her hold it up to her face and inhale. "The snow here smells good," she said, before tossing it down onto the ice, where it broke into a powder. "I'd get sad about her when I was younger, just so you know." She looked at me seriously. "Really sad. But now I just get angry."

At that moment, a figure emerged on the far shore of the lake. My cousin perked up immediately, her back rigid and straight. She narrowed her eyes against the light. "There's a person," she whispered.

"Probably just here to test the ice," I said, though a prickle of worry had come into my gut. I'd never before seen anybody appear on the other side of the water's edge.

"On Christmas Eve?"

"Maybe they live nearby. There's a sugar shack out that way." I pointed eastward, where I knew there were a couple dozen buckets nailed to maple trunks and a small sap house, but it wasn't the season. Not until February, at least. Elna nodded warily, her sight trained on the figure. The person moved steadily toward the ice line and then paused, lifting one foot down onto the surface and holding it there for a moment, waiting.

"They're going to walk on the lake," I said. "We have to warn them." I took a breath, poised to raise my arms in the air and shout, but Elna snatched my hand and lowered it back down with some force.

"Don't say anything," she hissed.

By then, the person had stepped fully onto the ice and was walking. He was still far away, maybe fifty or sixty feet, but we could tell now that it was a man. He wore a red-and-black flannel jacket and a skullcap with a scarf wrapped around his lower face. Elna had taken on the posture of a startled deer, her knees slightly bent as if she was ready to run. The worry in my stomach intensified. I abandoned any idea that this was someone sent by the town to measure the thickness of the ice. He carried no instruments, no clipboard. He took wide, unsteady steps. He paused for a moment, doubling over as if in pain, before continuing across the ice.

"That's Tom," Elna said.

"Are you sure?" I asked, surprised. She sounded so certain of it.

"Yes."

"How do you know?"

"I sewed a patch on that jacket." I looked out over the lake, shielding my eyes from the light. My pulse quickened. I did remember seeing one just like it in her mending pile.

"How can you tell it's the same jacket?" I asked. Elna didn't say anything. She just stood there in that same position, like she might bolt at any moment, watching.

I was starting to feel sick with dread but felt somehow protected by the height of the dock. We stood about eight feet above the ice where he walked. He paused again, crouching down with his hands on his knees, before abruptly lunging to his feet and ripping his hat off his head, shoving it down into one of his pockets. He grabbed at the top of his head with his fingers like there were bugs crawling on his scalp. I saw his hair then, uncovered. Blond curls.

"That is Tom," I said, sure of it now myself.

"Yes," Elna said in a clipped voice. "I told you."

"What's he doing out here?" For some reason, I cupped my hand partially over my mouth as I spoke, like a cartoon character in an exaggerated whisper. I felt immediately stupid, and forced my hands to rest stiffly at my sides. I then felt even more stupid that in this moment, when something frightening was happening, I was at all worried about how I looked.

"I bet he's stealing from the new site," Elna said. "It's out that way, right?" I nodded, my mouth dry. "I overheard some of them talking about how most of the equipment's been hauled in already," she explained. "One industrial winch is worth like, ten thousand dollars."

"A winch is pretty big," I said. "How could he get it out of here?"

"Well, maybe he's lifting engine parts, or like, copper wires from the machinery, I don't know," Elna hissed. "He's obviously high."

We looked at him. He was standing with his arms limply down at his sides, his head turned toward the site. He reached into his back pocket and pulled out a slim glass bottle and drank from it like a child, both hands gripping the sides. When it was empty, he tossed it down on the ice, where it spun around a few times before skidding to a stop in a patch of snow. I heard him laugh. I saw his teeth glinting at the edges of his mouth as he turned to look down at the bottle, giving it a sharp kick before continuing on over the ice. He stumbled a bit. One of his boots was untied, the laces flapping sadly behind him with each step.

"We should go," I said. I thought we could disappear back into the woods without a sound. I thought maybe he was walking on the ice out of confusion, or that someone had spotted him sniffing around the new lumber zone and chased him away. I thought he hadn't noticed us.

But then, I heard him say, "I see you girls." He didn't quite shout it, but the wind had settled and we could make the words out. He didn't seem angry, or friendly. There was no discernible tone at all. Just a voice carrying over the ice. *I see you girls.*

"Fuck," Elna breathed. The color had drained out of her face completely. She looked half dead. Tom lifted his arm in a strange, slow kind of wave, turning his hand back and forth in our direction. His shirt and jacket came up above his waistband as he reached, and there tucked into his pants was a loop of cable rolled flat against his bare skin. I narrowed my eyes at it, trying to get a clear view. He was still about thirty feet away, but I could see that it looked familiar. I thought it was the same kind of wire I'd seen hooked onto the jaws of a skidder. Galvanized steel, braided. He went to adjust it and the sun glinted against the metal. "See?" Elna whispered. "He has something."

As Tom moved, the cable came loose from his waistband and fell down onto the ice. It slid a few feet in front of him, where it all began to unravel like a snake uncoiling from its nest. Elna took a quick step back, startled. I watched as he lumbered forward, his scarf hanging loose around his shoulders, face red and contorted into a snarl. He gathered the wire up in his hands and twisted it back into a messy bundle, shoving it half down the front of his jeans. We just kept standing there, frozen in place, staring. He looked up, the hem of his jacket caught in the cable, and met our gaze. He remained still for a moment. His hand resting on the stolen equipment. He watched us watching him.

Then, Tom broke into a sudden run toward us. After a moment, he slipped and caught himself, coasting with his hands out at his sides in a wobbly struggle for balance. Before I could form a full thought, Elna darted down the length of the dock. I turned and saw her stop at the old firepit. She lifted up a rock, held it to her chest, and then slid it down toward me along the dock's slick surface. She hauled two more over, panting heavily. These rocks were not small. About the size of early watermelons. She pushed the three of them in a row before our feet and then grabbed my hand, squeezing it hard.

"What are you going to do with these?" I asked.

"I don't know," she said. "But we have to do something."

"We should run back down the trail," I told her. "Now."

"He'll catch up to us," she said.

"Not if we run right now." I turned to go, but Elna kept her grip firm on my hand.

Tom was now about fifteen feet away, drawing nearer with each passing moment. I heard him shout, "Girls!" in a drawling singsong. He'd seemed to figure out a way to walk without slipping, lifting each foot high in the air before bringing it down flat, arms outstretched. "How can I know you won't go talking about seeing me up here? How can I make sure of that?"

"We need to leave," I cried, trying to pull my cousin along. Elna let go of my hand and squatted down, lifting one of the rocks and grunting as she held it to her chest. She stood up and threw it off the end of the dock. It landed with an awful thud, not far from Tom. He stopped. Barely a second later, I heard the faint creak of splitting ice. He stood there with his palms straight out like he was willing the crack from growing. All three of us stared at the rock, motionless. The creaking stopped.

Tom looked up at us, a messy grin spread over his face. "That wasn't very nice," he shouted. "I know you still have some of my shit. I was going to let you keep it. Christmas present." He let out a wet chuckle. "But now I think you need to pay me for it." He started moving toward us again. He seemed emboldened, with a quicker gait.

Elna made a sound like a wounded animal and bent down, lifting the second rock up to her chest. She threw it down hard.

This time, it landed closer to Tom and broke through the ice instantly. A dark, shining hole appeared. Gently rippling water. He jumped to the side, the smile disappearing from his face. He slipped and fell, landing on his elbows, causing the ice to crack in another spot. Another rift formed, and then, within seconds, he was chin-deep in the water, gasping at the surface and reaching frantically toward the sky. I clapped my hand over my mouth. I could hear the sound of my own blood rushing in my ears. My feet felt bound to the dock. Elna said nothing. I watched her stare ahead, expressionless, as the pieces of shattered ice began floating back toward one another. I could see how easily it would re-form, seal itself up again, once all this was over.

Tom made several desperate attempts to haul himself out, breaking more ice each time. Elna held her arm across my chest as if to keep me in place. But there wasn't any possibility of me fleeing at that point, or even screaming for help. I could barely keep myself standing upright. There was a deep stabbing pain in my chest. My arms were almost completely numb. All I could do was watch his face, obscured by wet hair and his scarf, dip in and out of the water. Every sound seemed to amplify in gruesome detail: a wet gurgle rising from his throat, Elna's quick breath, a sudden gust of wind howling through the snowcapped pines.

Soon, Tom grew stiff and let go of the ice completely. He floated upright for a few moments, spinning like a buoy, still blinking, before gradually sinking below the surface and out of our view completely.

Elna dropped her arm from my chest. She stepped all the way

up to the very edge of the dock. I watched her use the toe of her boot to nudge the third rock over the side. It plopped glumly through the ice, down through the frigid darkness, past the frozen ropes of pondweed and star grass, deep down to where the snapping turtles slept.

15

I don't remember leaving the lake or walking back down the mountain. I don't remember the road back home, or going through the front door of the shop, or taking my coat off, or stomping the snow from my boots.

The next thing I can remember is sitting at the dining room table with Elna and Jen and my mother. There was the prime rib on a big platter in the center. Rolls, pureed potatoes, green beans in a soupy casserole with sliced almonds on top, roasted onions, yams topped with broiled marshmallows, thick gravy in a ceramic boat. I remember Jen cutting the meat, laying a slice onto everyone's plate, and a scraggly little pine tree in the corner with some colored lights strung around it. *Cut from Jen's yard,* I heard my mother say. I could smell the sap, the blood from the beef, the butter in the potatoes, cinnamon and vanilla from the kitchen mingling with the gas oven.

And there was Elna, sitting upright and smiling, her shoulders tall and straight. I remember the way her face looked. A clear, pretty smile. Polite questions. Bright eyes. She ate a whole plate of food and then got herself seconds. I could barely choke down half of mine. Jen was watching me from the sides of her eyes, I noticed, so I took a big bite of potato and let it sit in my mouth, waiting until my stomach felt calm enough to manage a swallow.

While I was waiting, my mother asked, "So what did you girls get up to out there?"

Before I could even blink, Elna spoke. "Ida took me to the five-and-dime," she said.

"Oh?"

"We had a nice stroll down there in the snow. I hardly ever get to see any snow." Her eyes were wide and sparkling. A sweet, girlish look fell across her face.

"Well, plenty out there now for you to enjoy." My mother took a big drink of her beer and placed the glass down with a thud. I winced at the sound.

"Hang on just one moment," Elna said, getting up from her seat. She scurried down to the spare room, returning a brief moment later with her hands full. In one hand was a small resin paperweight shaped like a pyramid with a penny suspended inside. In the other, a thumb-sized bottle of perfume. She placed the items before Jen and my mother. "I asked Ida to take me somewhere I could get you both some Christmas presents. I just wanted to say thank you for letting me be here, Aunt Anne." She stood at the table's edge as she spoke, leaning forward with both her hands pressed flat on the surface. It reminded me of the way a detective would stand in a TV show, questioning someone but being nice about it. The three of us sat there, looking back at her. I got the feeling no one quite knew what to say.

Finally, my mother spoke. "That's very sweet of you, Elna. Thanks."

Jen nodded, picking up the paperweight and turning it around, looking through its prism. My cousin took her seat again, this time sitting with her knees curled up to her chest and her head resting against them like a much younger girl. I felt a sudden urge to vomit and tried not to look at the red slab of meat sitting at the center of the table, fat turning solid at the surface of the pooled juice. I guessed Elna had taken these things when she got my key chain. I could picture where the paperweight had come from. There was a big display by the door with identical clear pyramids, all with different trinkets frozen inside.

I had Christmas presents for Jen and my mother, too, wrapped in tinfoil decorated with star-shaped stickers, sitting inside my desk in my room. I'd made both their presents at the beginning of the month when I was sitting out gym in the library. I'd found a book on pop-up papermaking in the stacks. It was old, maybe from the 1960s, written by a lady who described herself on the jacket as the grandmother of American pop-up books. I had no idea what that was supposed to mean, but I found the diagrams intriguing. I went into what was meant to be the computer lab, but was really just a room full of supplies and furniture that didn't fit anywhere else in the school. Every year they said we'd be getting computers, and that we'd all be learning how to type on a word processing program, but it never happened. I sifted through a big box of extra art supplies, taking a pair of scissors and some glue and a stack of thick card stock in different colors. I followed the instructions to make a pop-up of a snowcapped mountain range, dotted with pine trees and lakes, like a miniature Mineral, for Jen, and one of a farmhouse with red shutters and flowering window boxes for my mother. I skipped the rest of my classes that day and stayed in the computer lab, opening and closing the pop-ups at a table in the back corner, content to watch the little paper worlds disappear again and again, neatly secreted away within a plain folded sheet.

I heard my mother say, "Aren't you hungry, Ida?" I'd been holding the same spoonful of potatoes out before me for some time, I realized. I nodded, then went through the motions of putting the spoon in my mouth. As I chewed, I thought of Elna's blood splattering over the potatoes earlier in the day, of my mother rinsing them in the sink, of the first moment we stepped outside into the cold.

"This is all so delicious, Aunt Anne," Elna said. "I just can't get enough of these yams." She scooped more onto her plate and ate quickly, scraping the remnants with the side of her fork. Jen agreed. The conversation then turned to Jen's work. Her voice sounded like it was coming to me from many miles away. I picked up every few words. Something about welding a faulty pin bore, soldering padlock plates onto the doors of a pair of skidders.

"It was actually up at the new timber field," she said. "Seems like they're having some problems with theft."

"Oh?" Elna said.

"There's a kind of converter in them that goes for a lot," Jen explained. Under the table, I dug my nails into the sides of my thighs as hard as I could. I pinched at my skin through my jeans until the pain grew bigger than my nervousness. I glanced up at my cousin. Her face was still and pleasant. She looked like a happy girl at a holiday dinner who knew nothing about anything going on at any timber field.

"Did you always want to be a welder?" Elna asked.

"No." Jen chuckled. "I wanted to be a vet for livestock." She grabbed a roll from the basket in the center of the table and tore it open, dragging half of it around in the prime rib juice. "I grew up on a small farm. I always liked taking care of the calves." I'd heard mention of this a couple times before. The farm was in Puyallup. Once Jen's parents died, she and her brother sold it, unable to take on the expense of running it themselves.

We took a drive down there before it changed hands. Jen was fine the whole way, joking with my mother and humming along to music. Then, when we pulled through the gates, she became very emotional. The brother was already there, waiting. He stood on the porch of the little house with his hands in his pockets. Before my mother and I were introduced to him, the two of them went inside together and stayed there for a while.

What's going on? I asked.

I believe they're saying goodbye to the house, my mother said. I didn't totally get that, but I could see that it mattered to Jen. Afterward, the four of us walked around the property. By then, the animals were all gone. A marshy, sweet smell hung in the air. We came upon an overgrown garden where, I was told, they grew fruits and vegetables only for their personal use as a family. This patch of dirt had produced radishes, turnips, pumpkins, watermelons, tomatoes, peppers, all manner of herbs. Now, it was wild and decrepit. Jen's brother stuck his hand in a bush and pulled out a handful of raspberries. He popped them in his mouth, bright juice trickling down his chin. Fat, yellow caterpillars chewed holes in the leaves.

When my mother went to clear the table, Elna stopped her, insisting she sit back. "You've worked so hard all day, let me and Ida take care of everything." She grabbed me by the elbow and yanked me up, motioning to the dish of beef. "You take that one, I'll grab the rest."

"Looks like your cousin's teaching you some manners," my mother said, chuckling, casting a sharp glance my way. A wave of anger welled up in my chest and crested at the base of my throat. It felt like all I did was try to learn the rules of the human world, watching carefully and doing the best imitation of a nice, normal girl as I could muster, and still always missing something I could never identify. I glared at the floor. When I looked up to follow Elna into the kitchen, I could see Jen frowning, looking between my cousin and my mother and me, a troubled wrinkle set between her eyebrows.

I wrapped the beef dish in plastic and set it down in the bottom of the fridge. I pressed my forehead to the inside of the door, closing my eyes, trying to leave the room for a moment, even if I could only do it in my mind. When I stood up, Elna was standing about an inch away from me, staring right into my eyes. She studied my face, looking carefully over every inch. I wasn't sure what to do. She wasn't smiling anymore, the way she had been at the table. But she didn't look mad, either. I felt like a frog trapped in a jar.

Finally, she said, "All cool?"

"Yeah," I said. My voice sounded dry and small.

"Good," Elna replied, giving me a slow look up and down. "Now you're going to rinse off these dishes while I start bringing the dessert in." She led me over to the sink by my elbow. She tilted her chin right up to my ear and whispered, "Then, after dessert, you're going to say you're tired and you're going to go to sleep."

I did what she said.

16

At around four-thirty in the morning, I wokc up to Elna sitting on the edge of my bed. I could see the outline of her face above me, hair glowing in a savage halo around her head, illuminated by the patio floodlight finding its way in through my window.

"We need to get out of here," she said, her voice low.

I rubbed my eyes. "What are you talking about?" I sat up, pulling the quilt around my shoulders. I switched on the night-light at my bedside. I could see now that Elna was fully dressed in a matching sweater and skirt. She wore the same boots she'd had on at the lake. The two green bags she'd first arrived with were sitting by the door, her mint-colored parka draped over them. She slipped the boots off and started to walk around my room in her socks.

"Where's your bag?" she asked.

"What bag?"

She rolled her eyes. "Your overnight bag, your suitcase, whatever."

"I don't have one." She frowned, looking around, then grabbed a half-full laundry sack near the closet and emptied it out onto the floor. She grabbed a few things off of hangers and dropped them in, before bringing the sack to me, pushing it against my chest. I set it to the side. "I don't understand," I said.

"I told you, we've got to go."

"But why?"

"Why do you think?" I looked at her. I had a lot of thoughts rushing in my head. Whether we would've been able to make it down the mountain without Tom catching up to us. If she'd had the idea with the rocks from the first moment she spotted him all the way at the lake's other end. Why I didn't just run. I could've pulled my hand away from her if I'd tried hard enough, I was sure. But I'd just stood there, like a deer in the middle of the road. I did things like that all the time and I hated that I did. I'd get so overwhelmed my body would just completely seize up and lose all contact with my brain. Sometimes it was so bad I couldn't even will a finger to move. I had all these thoughts, but I didn't want to say any of them aloud.

"Look, I thought about it," Elna whispered. "And we have no way of knowing whether anybody saw us from the other side of that lake." She sat down on the bed and leaned in close to me. I could feel her hot breath on my neck. "Your mom's girlfriend said the company people know there's problems out at that field. If Tom ran out and wound up on the ice because some guy on watch duty chased him . . ." Her voice trailed off. "You understand what I'm saying?" she asked. A cold chill settled in my gut. I wished I was dreaming. For a moment, I wondered if there was any possibility that I *was* dreaming. That I had been since the moment Elna first walked in the door, and I might wake up to a world where she'd never reemerged into my life.

"So," she went on. "The best thing we can do is just leave now. Just for a while."

"I can't just *leave.*"

"You want to stay here?" Elna asked, snapping her head around. Her eyes were narrowed. I could see them shining in the dark. "Go back to school? Have to see that creepy guidance counselor every day?"

"No," I said. "But—"

"Get suffocated on the bus again?" she interrupted. "Or maybe next time it'll happen in the girls' bathroom?"

"I can't—"

She cut me off once more. "You want to stick around and see how much worse it gets for you?" I looked down at the quilt to avoid her stare. "When's your winter break over?" she asked.

"Next week," I said, my pulse already beginning to quicken with dread just thinking about it.

"Just think." She put on a fake, cheerful voice, leaning in close to me as she spoke. "Only a few more days before you get to visit Mr. Carter. I bet you can't wait for him to study you like you're some retarded lab rat, taking his secret notes, reporting back home on all your *progress.*"

My eyes began to sting. People called me that word all the

time. Not just kids at school. Adults, too. When I couldn't tell left from right, when I couldn't do buttons. Often when I just asked too many questions. I thought of a time that fall when I'd been standing in a line with all the other freshmen in the hallway by the nurse's station. She had us come up to a little curtained-off area one by one, checking our spines for scoliosis and measuring our height. When it was my turn, I stood in front of her, studying the creases in her lavender eye shadow as she flipped the page on her clipboard.

"Lift your shirt and bend your back," she said, still looking at the paper.

"Which way?" I asked.

"What?" She glared up at me. Her lower eyelashes were thickly coated in mascara, carefully separated into individual hairs. I wondered if she used a needle to separate them. I'd seen a movie where a woman did that.

"Which way do I bend?"

"What are you, retarded?" she spat. "Lean forward so I can see your back."

The word rang in my ears for the rest of the day. Every time I heard it, it echoed. Every time I heard it, the well of anger in my chest grew deeper and wider.

"I don't want to go back to school," I finally said, taking a slow breath and trying to steady myself. "But I can't, like, run away."

"Why not? You're fourteen. Almost fifteen. Your birthday is in just a few weeks, right? That's only three years away from legal adulthood. You aren't a little kid anymore."

"Yeah, but my mother," I said. "She'll freak out."

"Who cares? She's always mad at you about something anyway, right?" Elna held her hand out before her, looking at her nails. She adjusted one of her rings, and then said, "You know you could never tell her what happened at the lake, right?"

"I know," I muttered.

"She wouldn't get it."

"I know that," I repeated.

"She doesn't get *you.*"

"Yeah, but she's still my mother."

"Your mother," Elna said, a little smile appearing on the corner of her lips. "You want to know something about your mother?" I looked at her, unsure if I should answer. It didn't have the sound of a real question. It had the sound of a challenge, or a game, like she was always going to tell me this *something,* but still wanted me to ask her for it anyway. I nodded slowly. "You sure?" she said. I wanted to kick her a little bit.

"What is it?" I asked, starting to feel kind of sick.

"You really sure?"

"What is it, Elna?" I asked again. For some reason, I got up out of the bed. I leaned against the wall, arms crossed over my stomach.

"Anne isn't even your mother, not really." She paused. "Candace is."

I didn't really understand what she'd said. I heard the words, I knew what each of them meant, but when my brain put them all together, no meaning came out. It was just sounds. I shook my head, squinting. "What are you saying? That doesn't make any sense."

"You really never wondered?" Elna asked.

"Of course I've never wondered. Why would I wonder that?" I walked over to my desk and sat down in the swivel chair. I started to spin very slowly.

"How did you think she got pregnant with you? Some old bull dyke like Jen?"

"Obviously, I know not like that," I said.

"So, then, who?"

"She told me it was unplanned, a guy she had a few dates with who moved to Calgary. She already knew she wanted to be a mother, so she decided to just go ahead and have me alone."

"Oh? What was his name?"

"I don't know."

"Have you seen a picture of him?"

"No," I said. "But so what?"

"*So,* none of that's true," Elna said, crossing her arms in front of her chest in a satisfied way.

"You're lying," I said. "You just want me to run away with you."

"That's got nothing to do with it. I don't give a shit if you believe me or not, because the truth is the truth. We have the same mom."

"We don't look alike," I said.

"I didn't say we were twins," Elna scoffed.

"It doesn't make any sense." I shook my head again. "Do you know the law of parsimony?" I asked.

"Oh my god," Elna groaned. "No."

"It's a principle that says the simplest explanation for something is the most reliable explanation."

"Okay."

"So, if I'm making the fewest possible assumptions, entertaining the least possible complicating factors"—I stopped swiveling and looked at her—"then I should think you're just making this up."

"Why would I make this up?"

"I already said, to get me to run away with you, because you did something stupid at the lake."

"*I* did something stupid?" she hissed. "I saved both our asses at the lake. You were just standing there with your mouth open."

"Fine, but I didn't do anything wrong," I said.

"You were there with me, weren't you?" She gave me an icy smile. "You watched everything happen. You didn't try to stop it." A ripple of nausea spread through my stomach. My palms felt damp. Elna tilted her head toward the ceiling and let out a long sigh. "But anyway, sure, let's go with this parsimony thing." She stood up and came over to the desk, setting her hand on top of a map of the Solomon Islands. She looked down at me. "What makes more sense, what's more simple?" She held both her hands out to either side like a scale. "Rug-munching Anne had a fling with some mystery guy who she never went after for child support, whose name you don't know, who never came back to visit or sent you anything on your birthday or has any other family around here who might want to meet you, who conveniently moved to another country and was never heard from again." She let out a little laugh. "*Or,* your real mom, too messed up to even take care of one kid, accidentally got knocked up a second time and gave the baby to her nice, normal, childless sister who had a real job with a cute little place in the country." I stared at the ground. "Look, we can talk about all this on the way," she said. "It's going to get light out soon." She slipped into her parka and picked up both of her bags. "I already grabbed your toothbrush and stuff."

"Where are we going?"

"Home to San Francisco."

I stood up and started dropping things into the laundry bag. I felt weirdly, suddenly calm. What if I did go with her? What could stop me? Just a few minutes ago the idea had seemed so impossible. Now, I felt myself being pulled toward it, like some invisible, magnetic force was pushing me along, moving my hands as I grabbed my deck of flag cards and a folder full of maps and tucked them inside the bag. Leaving still seemed a little crazy, a little scary. But it didn't really seem worse than what I was already facing. I thought about how it would feel to walk back into the school building just a week from now. The smell of the guidance counselor's office. The buzzing overhead lights. What other kids might do to me. It wouldn't get any better coming home at the end of the day now, either. Not anymore. What if people started asking about Tom? What if the police showed up? And I'd just have to sit there, pretending I didn't know where he really was. And when my mother looked at me, I'd have to look back at her face, knowing what Elna had just told me. The idea of it all made my heart pound. Then I tried to imagine how it would feel to just leave all of it behind. Just drive away. I yanked a handful of underwear from my top drawer and tossed them in the bag along with the pot of silver eye glitter. I packed all the clean socks I could find, and then grabbed my favorite pair of corduroy pants.

"You still have that weird birthmark on your back?" Elna asked. I nodded, looking up at her warily. It was in between my shoulder blades. The shape of a kidney bean. "When we get there, I'll show you a picture that'll prove I'm not bullshitting you."

I put my coat on and then pulled a piece of loose-leaf from one of my binders. I set the paper down on the desk and looked at it, pen in hand, hesitating. I felt like I should leave a note, but I wasn't sure what to say. I put the pen down, picked it up, then placed it down again. I glanced at my packed bag and bit my lip. Nothing felt right. Nothing made sense.

Elna seemed to pick up on my moment of indecision. "Clock's ticking," she said. "You can come with me, or, if you want, you can stay here and wait to see what happens."

I grabbed the pen and scribbled, simply, *Elna told me everything.* I left the paper on my pillow, slung my bag over my shoulder, and followed her out the door.

17

We moved quietly around the back of the house and into the Arthurs' driveway.

Patrick's car was parked in its usual spot. The same mess of CDs littered the dashboard. Elna pulled a set of keys from her pocket and opened the driver's door, pressing her hand over the lock to muffle any noise. I kept looking back and forth between the windows at my house and our neighbors'. No light. No movement. The sky was still full of stars. She tossed our bags into the backseat and ushered me around to the passenger's side, pushing me in and closing the door carefully. Once she was behind the wheel I asked her where she got the keys.

"I saw where he keeps them," she explained. "He just hangs them on a hook in the garage, by the door. You can see it from your yard."

"How did you get in, though?"

"He left the door unlocked," she said, shrugging. I thought of Patrick, probably asleep just feet from us at that moment. Later in the morning, Christmas morning, he would wake up to find his car gone.

"Can't we just take a bus?" I said. "That's how you got here."

"There aren't any today. I looked at the schedule. Besides, we can't be hanging around the bus stop, waiting."

"Patrick didn't do anything to us, though."

"No," she agreed. "But we need a car." She backed out of the driveway. "He has insurance, probably. He'll report it stolen, and they'll pay for a replacement. It's fine. It's good, actually. He'll get a new car out of it."

When we turned onto the road out of Mineral, passing by the town sign and getting on the interstate, something came over me. It was a feeling that moved quickly throughout my whole body, like a fire, spreading in an instant to the tips of my fingers and over the roof of my mouth, down into the bottoms of my feet. I looked back at the town sign in the side mirror, the fading blue paint getting smaller and smaller, population one thousand and eight hundred, and the feeling came at me hard and fast. I knew I would never forget what it felt like to drive away from home for the first time. Even while it was happening, even in that moment, I knew it.

Some kind of seal had been broken beyond repair. Mineral would never be the same again. This place, the only place in the world I really knew, a place I didn't love and didn't hate and felt I understood as much as I could hope to understand any place, had been turned entirely upside down. I thought of the first moment

Elna walked into the shop, the way she shook the snow out of her hair. I thought of Tom walking on the ice. How his voice rang out over the lake, echoing against the trees. How he struggled, thrashing, before going still. We drove past the turnoff to my school, and I thought of the pink liquid soap in the bathroom dispensers and the strange smell it had. Like apple juice mixed with bleach. And the globe in the library with its bumpy, papered surface. The globe in my room, which I'd gotten from a catalog with money I'd won at a geography competition. The little globe on the desk of Dr. Fields' office, and his droning lectures about minding my defective heart, and his cold, pale, liver-spotted hands. I started to think of my mother and Jen, asleep, some miles back down the road, but it hurt too much so I stopped.

The blue light of dawn began to emerge on the horizon. A flock of birds cut through the sky in a dark arrow. "You want to know what I think?" Elna said.

"What?"

"I think Anne was kind of hoping I would tell you." I looked over at her. She was leaning toward the window, driving with one hand on the wheel and the other resting on her temple.

"That's ridiculous," I replied.

"No, it's really not." She paused for a moment, staring out ahead at the road. She cleared her throat. "So, she has this big secret about you, right? And every year she probably thinks about telling you the truth, but then bitches out and tells herself she'll wait one more year to talk to you about it. Probably tells herself you're still too young to know. It's a good excuse for her. Like, to tell herself it's about your maturity or whatever and not about her lacking the guts to just be honest. But then as more years go by, it becomes this bigger, scarier thing. The idea of telling you intimidates her more and more. What if you freak out at her? What if you're mad she didn't tell you sooner? You're getting into your teens, you're moody, and she doesn't really get you and your whole deal anyway." Elna waved her driving hand loosely around in the air for a moment as she said the word *deal,* leaving the wheel unattended, as if she wanted to be more specific but wasn't quite sure how to say it. I didn't blame her for that. I wasn't always sure how to explain myself, either.

Elna continued, "So, she keeps chickening out. Maybe has some idea to reveal it all on your eighteenth birthday or something dramatic like that. But then I come along. And she probably worries that I'm going to tell you. I know she does, because she gave me this weird, vague warning about it when I first showed up. But that was a trick, right? She was a teenager once. She knows if she tells me not to, I'm likely to do it even more. And either way she wins. Because if I don't say anything, then whatever. Fine. Business as usual. But if I do, then it takes all that buildup and anxiety away from her. No more pressure, no more big secret."

Elna took a long breath and then let out a strange, short laugh before adding, "And the best part for her is that *I* get to be the bad guy. I'm the one who blew the lid off this whole thing, I'm the one who did what I wasn't supposed to do. Every finger can be pointed right at me for stirring the pot. And when the initial shock wears off, and you inevitably start to ask questions about why she didn't tell you herself any sooner, she can feed you some carefully crafted bullshit about how she had a whole plan to do it once you reached a certain age, and she just wanted the time to be right, and it's all my fault for ruining what was going to be a special moment. But there never was a plan, there wasn't going to be any precious moment, she was always gonna be too chicken-shit to be honest with you." Elna chuckled. "You should really be thankful that I came along when I did. Who knows when you would've learned the truth."

Her whole speech left me feeling a little sick in my stomach. I wasn't sure exactly what to think. Mostly, it didn't seem that far-fetched. It didn't sound *unlike* my mother. We drove in silence for a while. As the trees blurred past, I started to think that if it was true, then I really was angry she didn't tell me herself a long time ago. If I'd always known, then it would never have been a big deal. It would've just been a fact of my life, somewhere in the mix with every other fact that wasn't exactly good or bad, but just *was.* Now, though, it could never be that way.

It felt like every thought in my brain was too big to manage. I wished I could unscrew my head from my body and toss it on the side of the road. I rolled the window down and leaned out as far as I could, inhaling the cold air deeply and keeping my eyes on the passing scenery. Tall green pine trees and moss-covered rocks. Some grazing deer. Highway signs. All of it coming to me in one fast blur. I could tell Elna kept looking over at me. I think she was trying to figure out what I was thinking, whether I thought she was telling the truth, if I wished I hadn't gotten in the car with her. I kind of liked that she wasn't sure. I closed my eyes and let the wind batter my face. It smelled like rain was coming.

I had this little spark of a thought that maybe what I was doing wasn't such an awful idea, running off like this. For years, most everyone around me wanted me to change, whether it was the tone of my voice or the way I greeted people when I walked into a room. If it wasn't that I needed to be less rigid, it was that I needed to smile more, or try new things, or stop spending so much time alone. They wanted me to be different than I really was, and they made sure I knew. So here I was, doing something different. I could feel the spark growing into a flame.

After a while I rolled the window up, opened the glove box, and began rooting around. "Anything good in there?" Elna asked. There was the vehicle registration with Patrick's name on it. I held it up to her. She looked at it, side-eyed, and then said, "Do me a favor and tear that up into a bunch of little pieces, then toss the pieces out the window, okay?" I did what she said. The paper left smudges of black ink on my fingertips. "Just in case we get pulled over," she added.

"Do you think we will?" I asked.

"We won't."

"But you just said we might."

"If he reports the car stolen, then maybe cops will be out looking for it. I think they'll be slower to respond to a nonemergency on Christmas, but we should get as far from Mineral as we can today."

"What if my mother reports us as missing?"

"Didn't you leave some kind of note? It's not illegal to run away."

"She could still call the police."

"Don't worry about that," she said. "What else has he got?" There was a small flashlight and a paper brochure for a cave kayaking tour with a phone number written on the front in blue pen, the name *Erica* scrawled above the digits. There were lemon cough drops and a loose black button. There was a twenty-dollar bill, too, which I discreetly folded up and pushed inside my sleeve.

"Any cash?" she asked.

"No," I said.

"That's okay, I have some." A moment later, "We need to stay off busy roads as much as we can. It's like, an eighteen-hour drive if we avoid the highways. I think we can do it in a couple days."

"Do you know the way?" I asked.

"I mean, kind of," she muttered, looking back over her shoulder as she merged into a new lane. "Does he keep a road map in there?" He did have one, and I unfolded it over half of the dashboard, leaning forward and looking at all the thin, tangled lines. A mess of arteries across the whole Northwest, all feeding into Seattle and Portland, fanning out and growing fainter, farther apart, near the southern edge of Oregon.

"Keep an eye out and let me know if we're on the right track," she said. "You should be good at that, right?"

"Yeah," I told her. "The big roads kind of trail off once you get into the top of California."

"Works for us." She let out a long yawn. "Once we pass a rest stop farther out, I'll get a coffee." She glanced at me. "I'm assuming you don't know how to drive?" I shook my head no. "That's okay," she said, reaching over and ruffling my bangs. "I can teach you sometime. How cute would that be, teaching my little sister how to drive?"

We wound our way through small towns, hugging the coast as closely as we could. I pressed my forehead against the window and looked at huge, jagged rocks rising out of the ocean, waves crashing against them, great jets of sea spray raining back down into the surf. There were lighthouses every so often. Sometimes I'd see a car with a pine tree roped to the roof. I spent a moment considering whether I cared that it was Christmas, and came up blank. I saw a huddle of sea lions on one stretch of sand, surrounded by curious gulls. Elna drove carefully, stopping at every light and minding the speed limit.

We pulled off at a desolate gas station where we got cups of coffee from a vending machine. The taste was awful. I took one sip before giving mine to Elna. We got bags of peanuts from the machine, too, and chocolate bars, and a package of barbecue potato chips. Humidity had found its way through the foil wrapping. The chips were soggy. I filled my hands with cold water from the drinking fountain and splashed my face. The fountain was just sitting in a patch of grass, away from the pumps. Little white flowers sprouted up from the surrounding earth, fed by the spout's continuous, low trickle. I drank, and then splashed my face again.

The hours passed. We listened to Patrick's CDs. I liked them. I'd never really listened to music on purpose before. I didn't have a stereo in my room or buy tapes or anything. Some of the jewel cases were on the floorboard and I looked through them, fascinated by the images on the covers. In one, a young boy, lit by a hazy orange glow, was gazing through a glass jar full of black flies. I put the disc in and let it play. When the second track began, it felt like a dozen flowers burst into full bloom, all at once, all in my brain. It was like the walls of my head expanded to make room for the sound. I couldn't believe what I was hearing. I turned the volume up. I'd never intentionally made sounds louder. But there'd never been anything like this before. I checked the back of the CD case to see what the song was called. "Nutshell." I turned the word over again and again like a coin, mouthing it silently into my lap. *Nutshell.* Each time it ended, I pressed the back arrow and started it once more.

"How many times are you going to play that?" Elna asked.

"This'll be the last time," I said. "I just really like it."

"Of course you do," she said.

"Why of course?"

"Just seems like your kind of thing." She leaned her elbow on the console and rolled her neck around, cracking the vertebrae. "I had a boyfriend who liked that band. He was so depressed all the time. Great artist, though. He drew me the coolest picture of a dragon with like, a woman's face? I think he wanted me to get a tattoo of it. He was a tattoo artist." She gave me a knowing glance, rolling her eyes quickly, as if I could relate in any way to the hassle of a sad, tattoo-artist boyfriend. "He ended up killing himself before he could give it to me, though."

18

After dark, we pulled off onto a side road in a state forest. We were somewhere south of Eugene, still right along the coast. The air tasted like sea salt, even inside the car. There weren't any lights, not even a streetlamp illuminating the forest's sign. We spotted the entrance as we passed by, and Elna abruptly shifted the car into reverse, maneuvering a tight turn to bring us back the other way.

"I should really get some sleep," she said. "It'll be empty in there."

It was empty. The trail grew narrow and uneven, winding through thickets of tall trees and ferns. I could hear the crunch of sand and fallen pine needles beneath the tires. We reached a gravel clearing, where there was a tsunami evacuation zone notice stapled to a spruce trunk and a rusty chain between two poles, dividing the empty lot from the shore cliff. Elna turned the engine off and we sat there for a while, quiet, beams dark, doors locked, just watching. Eventually, she said, "I think this'll be okay."

We lay awake with the seats down. Elna found some of Patrick's jackets and an old blanket in the trunk and spread them out. I could feel every lump of a seat belt and loose coin under me, even through the layers. It was the first time I'd ever spent the night anywhere but my own bed in Mineral. I tried to sleep, but every time I closed my eyes there came a slideshow of everything that had happened since Elna's arrival. The electric feeling of her pressing the stolen mood ring into my palm, all the way to the sound of the ice cracking on the lake. When I reached the end of the slideshow, it started over again. Faster and faster each time.

From somewhere in the dark near me, I heard Elna ask, "Why aren't you sleeping?"

"I don't know," I said. "Why aren't you?"

"We're in the middle of nowhere. It's weird out here." I lifted my head up and looked out the rear window. Nothing but black air. I knew we were close to the ocean. I knew there were trees. Boulders dotting the line where the sand met the dirt lot. But it just felt like we were floating in space and the car was our rocket ship.

"When I try to sleep, I think about Tom," I said. "And then I can't sleep."

"Why are you doing that?" I felt her turn toward me.

"I don't know."

"What do you think would've happened if I'd let him get all the way to the dock?"

"I don't know," I said. I did have an idea, of course. But I didn't want to talk about it.

"It wouldn't have been good. It would have been worse than what ended up happening."

We lay there for a while, quiet. I could hear her breathing. I could hear the wind coming in off the sea. Finally, she said, "Candace and I used to sleep in parking lots." I noticed that sometimes Elna said *Candace* and other times she said *Mom.* I tried to find patterns between her mood and the tone of her voice, and which one she used. "She'd get these ideas that we were going to leave San Francisco and start over somewhere else," Elna explained. "We'd go scout out these other places, sometimes for a couple weeks at a time. Las Vegas, Phoenix, Albuquerque. A bunch of different towns."

"Did you like any of them?"

"Vegas was okay. Kind of depressing, I guess. But the food was good."

"How did you know what parking lots to stay in?"

"Places that were open overnight, like a diner or a big supermarket. No bars. We had a van then. I mean it wasn't ours but we were using it all the time. There was a mattress in the back and curtains on the windows so at least no one could look in at us sleeping. I was always finding porn and old chicken bones under the seats. Such a gross van, honestly. I don't even know who it really belonged to."

She told me about going to a place in Arizona where Candace thought she might be able to find a job. Hazy visions of cacti and long, golden stretches of desert formed in my mind. The first morning they were there, she said, Candace dropped her off at the local public school.

"She just pulled around to the front and told me she'd come back at the end of the day. I was like, *You're crazy, I don't even have a pencil.* So she dug a pen out of the glove box and gave it to me and sent me inside." I listened as Elna described going into the first classroom she saw, every pair of eyes settling on her in confusion. I could imagine it. I mean, I knew what it was like to feel that you didn't belong at school and to have everyone staring at you, sneers just on the edges of their lips. If it were me, I thought, I would've hid somewhere outside for the rest of the day, waiting silently. But Elna told me she decided in that moment to just make up a story. She was Amanda from Texas. She'd just moved to town. Could she please borrow a couple sheets of paper from someone?

"The teacher just said okay?" I asked.

"She was surprised, at first. She said she didn't have me on her roster. But I told her my parents were still in the office, finishing up my enrollment. And then I just sat down at an empty desk."

"What if you ended up actually moving there, though? And everyone found out your name wasn't really Amanda?"

"I knew that wasn't going to happen," she said. She let out a sound like a sigh and a laugh pressed together. "It was weird, I was just sitting there all day in these classrooms taking notes on photosynthesis and the Constitution or whatever with borrowed paper. I had lunch with this group of girls. One of them invited me to her fucking pool party that weekend. And I told her I would come."

"Did you go?"

"No, we left the next day."

Enough time passed silently that I thought she might have fallen asleep, but then I heard her say, "You know, one time Mom had this idea that we were going to come get you. We made it all the way up near Reno." A little twinge shot through my heart. Like a needle piercing its way through.

"What happened?" I asked.

"We pulled into a Jack in the Box parking lot to sleep for the night. She kept talking about how it was time to have you back, that it had been long enough. She kept asking me if it was going to be okay, wanting to know if I was ready for it. I told her it was fine. She seemed pretty serious about it. When the sun came up we went inside to wash off in the bathroom and have breakfast, but when we got back in the van she turned south on the highway and we went straight home to San Francisco."

"When was this?" I asked.

"This was only a couple years ago," Elna said. I wasn't sure how to respond, so I didn't, and eventually we both drifted off to sleep.

19

I woke up in the morning to find Elna leaning on the hood of the car, brushing her teeth and spitting onto the sand. Sitting up on my elbows in the back, I could see the ocean rolling out into the far distance. A gauzy layer of fog hung over the cliff brush and the trees, stretching over the water where the waves broke. Yesterday felt like a trance I'd fallen hard into, now broken by the daylight. I'd half expected to wake up to police or park rangers, or even Jen and my mother, or the woman I'd only ever known as my mother, knocking at the windows, hysterical. But there were just morning birds, and the soft sound of crashing water many feet below. Stark, gray light. No one knew where we were. There wasn't anyone around to care. Elna had already changed into new clothes and brushed her hair out. She had her makeup bag with her, and was angling a small mirror around her face, gliding a dark pencil over her eyelids.

Watching her, I noticed a strange, burning fascination. It was different than before. I'd been a little taken with Elna since she showed up, but that was because of her polished fingernails, and her magazine clothes, and the way she carried herself with such an unflappable, icy confidence. Now, suddenly, I was mesmerized by the very material of our bodies. I zeroed my gaze in on her wrist, studying the smooth roll of her joint as she flicked the pencil, the narrow taper of her forearm. I imagined the pulse of her veins and the marrow of her bones. I wanted to know whether she had any birthmarks, like I did, or if her littlest toenail disappeared into a sunken crescent, too. I couldn't believe that there was this other girl in the world, whose existence I'd been only so vaguely aware of, who was half of me. How might things have been different if we'd grown up together, as sisters?

I started to imagine a completely different life. A girlhood outside of Mineral. Maybe Elna was right about the schools in San Francisco. Maybe everything would have been easier for me there. I knew Candace was always having a hard time, but what if I could have somehow helped? Or what if we'd both been given away, sent to Washington to be raised together? If I'd had Elna around, I probably wouldn't have needed to spend so much time trying to learn smiles from magazine pictures, I thought. She would've shown me how to act in the world. And if she lived with us, she wouldn't have had to spend all her time trying to take care of Candace. She wouldn't have had so much to worry about, trying to fill out forms for caseworkers and socking away escape money. In the summers, we could have swum together in the crisp, blue lake water. It wouldn't have been ruined.

After a while, Elna turned around, catching my eye through the windshield. We looked at each other, not blinking, or pretending to suddenly be busy with something else. I had the feeling she was having the same kind of thoughts as me.

Driving out to the main road, we passed a couple of campers with families inside, pulling all their gear into the park. One of the dads gave a little wave to Elna from behind the dashboard, and she waved back. Once we'd gotten some distance, she asked me, "Can you look at the map?"

"We're approximately here," I told her, pointing to a wide bend in the road a little ways west of a town called Drain. She glanced at it.

"If we drive all day today, then we can get there tomorrow afternoon."

"All right," I said. I'd had a bad dream the night before about getting to San Francisco and there being nothing. Just piles of ash and rubble where the city once was. "How do you know she's home?" I asked. Elna didn't answer right away. I added, "Candace, I mean." She nodded a little, looking out at the road quietly.

A couple miles later she said, "If she isn't, it's fine. I have keys. We'll just wait."

"I don't know what to say to her," I said.

"What?"

"I don't know what to say when I see her."

"It doesn't matter," she said. "She'll just be happy to see you there."

"Really?"

"Yeah," Elna muttered. A gloomy look passed over her face and settled there for a little while. She gripped the steering wheel tightly.

We took a long, flat road that ran parallel to the sea, level with the shore. There were people out on the sand in big coats and duck boots, walking against the brisk wind. A few of them had dogs. The dogs ran to fetch sticks of driftwood, bounding back toward their owners, all four feet leaving the ground. Every so often, we passed a logging truck and my chest would seize up. I'd spot them from far down the road. Massive stacks of stripped trunks, rattling around in the caged flatbed. Gray vapor trailing from the smokestack on the cab. Elna passed these trucks quickly, keeping her face away from the driver's view.

"Turn around and act like you're reaching for something in the backseat," she'd say. I listened. She said she thought she was probably being overkill, that by now we were pretty far from Washington, but I knew that some of the loggers wound up driving the timber far distances. Southern California, Texas, Colorado. Some of them even took cross-country routes.

In the afternoon, we came upon a stretch of beach with a small paved lot. There was a snack cart set up near the steps down to the sand. An old man stood next to it. He wore a pair of padded flannel overalls and a western hat secured around his chin with a cord. Elna pulled in. There were no other cars parked. She yanked a beanie over her head, tucking all her red hair up inside of it.

"Here," she said. "Put these on, just in case." They were her white sunglasses, the ones I'd admired when she first arrived. On my face, they looked cartoonishly big. We approached the cart.

The air was cool and muggy. We'd long since left behind any snow. Here, tall reeds grew along the dunes. The old man didn't seem interested in us. He stood there, looking at a gull picking at a scrap of bread. There were bananas in a bowl. Some hard, small oranges. He had Pop-Tarts, and a stack of road maps, and some jumper cables in a plastic bag. There was a piece of cardboard that read, *Coffee, 1$.* Elna bought two strawberry Pop-Tarts and asked him for a cup with sugar. He went to the back of the cart and pulled out a big camping thermos, pouring her coffee into a paper cup with a flimsy-looking lid.

He then held up a blue Gatorade and said simply, "Fifty cents."

We took everything down the steps onto the beach, where there were some benches looking out over the water. I kept noticing the side of Elna's mouth as she ate, the way her upper lip curved together in the middle. The sharp point of her chin.

"Did Candace tell you to bring me back?" I asked.

"We talked about it."

"And?"

"She was worried about upsetting her sister." Elna took a long drink of coffee. "But then she was so sick and out of it at that point, I'm not sure she even remembers now. We didn't have a plan or anything." I opened the Gatorade and drank it all down in a few gulps. I hadn't realized how thirsty I'd been. "Things just got fucked up and now here we are," she said, crossing her arms over her stomach and leaning back on the bench. "I didn't think I'd be bringing you anywhere." She cast me a sharp, quick look. I worried that maybe she'd begun to wish she hadn't woken me up after bed on Christmas Eve. We ate quietly for a while, then I got up from the bench and walked to the shoreline.

Swells rose and fell in the distance. Veils of mist whipped off the crests and evaporated before my eyes. Somewhere far down on a distant part of the beach, a fisherman cast a long line. I removed my boots and walked in a little farther. The water was cold but it didn't bother me. Sea foam washed around my ankles. Even though I did kind of want to see San Francisco, and I kind of wanted to see Candace again, too, I wished very much that I could just keep walking into the ocean. I imagined going farther and farther until my toes didn't touch the bottom, and the waves lifted me up, carrying me along, far away from the human world.

20

At around ten at night, we pulled into a town called Eureka. It was the biggest place for miles, the only one with any lights you could see from a distance. Elna slowed the car down on the main road and started scanning around for restaurants that still looked open. Some men sat down on the curb in a row, smoking. A dog loped across the street, something hanging out of its mouth. Halfway down, we spotted a tavern on the corner with a big, neon sign above the door that read *Sadie's*. In smaller letters underneath: *Bar, Food, Billiards.* The sound of many people laughing and shouting spilled out every time the door swung open to let someone in or out.

Elna parked the car across the way and said, "Just follow me. Don't talk to anyone." I wouldn't have, even without her asking. My brain felt like a piece of pounded meat after so many hours of driving. I could still feel the rumbling of the car's engine reverberating through my body. My legs tingled, blood rushing back into the numbness.

A burst of warm air, heavy with grease and smoke, hit us as we walked inside the tavern. I stayed close behind as we made our way past the crowd waiting to place food orders in the front, then past the bar with its full row of red vinyl seats, past the cluster of booths littered with pitchers of beer and spilled fries, and the pool tables where pairs of men shouted at each other, cues raised in the air, and the television screens, and the jukebox, and the Happy Days pinball machine. All the noise was making my teeth hurt. I balled up my hands, digging my nails into the flesh of my palms.

I followed her all the way to the back, into the ladies' room. No one else was in there. It smelled like artificial fruit. There was a metal napkin dispenser bolted to the wall with a big, fist-shaped dent in it. I leaned back against the sink and watched as Elna fished around inside the wastepaper basket with her bare hand, pulling out a crumpled receipt and flattening it out against the countertop next to me.

"We'll go out and get something to eat in a minute," she said. "It won't take long."

I nodded.

"Are you all right?" she asked.

"Fine," I told her.

"You're even quieter than usual."

"Just tired," I replied, even though it wasn't that simple.

"Yeah, me too." She wiped the mascara smudges from under her eyes and bit her bottom lip. She looked like she was thinking about something. After a couple minutes she said, "Let's sleep somewhere decent tonight. I saw a motel on the way in—we'll go there after this." She looked in the mirror, fluffing up her hair and reapplying a coat of lip gloss, before taking me by the arm, the receipt from the trash in her other hand, and bringing me back out into the restaurant.

We stood near the pickup counter with many other people, all jostling and chatting, holding receipts in their hands. Elna kept a close eye on what baskets of food were placed out. Five orders were picked up by the people in the front. We stood there, waiting, until one of the numbers was called out twice. Elna waited just a moment after the second call, then took a step forward and snatched the tray confidently, smiling at the guy behind the counter. He smiled back vacantly as we shuffled quickly through the crowd and left through the front door, food in hand.

We sat on a bench a little ways down the street, near where we'd parked. Elna handed me a cheeseburger wrapped in greasy wax paper. I devoured it. I realized then how desperate I'd been for real, hot food. There was a bridal shop across the street, the mannequins in its window display illuminated under harsh spotlights that spilled out onto the sidewalk, casting a yellow tinge over the ground. The mannequins were all tall and lean, with heavy painted-on makeup. Two blond wigs and a brunette. The one in the center wore an enormous, cream-colored gown with long lace sleeves and puffs on each shoulder. She had a veil that dropped down her back and came all the way around to the floor, pooling at the hem of her dress in gauzy ripples. Behind the mannequins, I could see the shadowy outlines of other gowns displayed on wall hooks, like ghosts all hung in a row.

"Do you want to get married one day?" I asked Elna.

She chewed slowly, thinking, before saying, "I probably will."

"You would look great in that one," I said, pointing to the window dress on the right. It was long and strapless, intricately beaded with swirling floral patterns and two elbow-length ivory gloves.

She nodded in agreement, then asked, "Do you think you'll get married?"

"Yes," I answered without hesitation, though it wasn't something I'd thought heavily on. We used to stock a bridal magazine on the rack at the store, and I'd never even paged through it, but still. I just had this feeling that there would be someone. I could sense it deep down. A hazy image on the far horizon that would someday, suddenly, shift into focus.

"What kind of guy?" Elna asked.

"Someone like Jen," I said. Again, without hesitation. That was just something I knew, too.

"Yeah," she replied. "I can see that."

We sat for a while longer on the bench, looking at the mannequins in the display, eating everything on the tray. Three orders of fries. They tasted like the best thing I'd ever had, even as I started to get full. People filtered in and out of bars on the street, laughing and smoking, looking for their cars.

At one point, a lady in a ratty old sweater appeared on the sidewalk next to us, digging through an old metal trash bin. She rifled through it with her bare hands and then, after not finding anything worth pulling out, knelt down on the asphalt and started picking up cigarette butts. She held each one up to the light of the streetlamp, checked for tobacco remnants in what remained of the paper casing. Some she tossed back, some she stuffed in a plastic grocery bag she held in the crook of her elbow. It had a big yellow smiley face on it. The word *THANKS* beneath. She was wearing red cowboy boots. They were dirty, and one heel seemed to be coming loose.

The lady noticed the two of us then and approached, hand outstretched. "Do you have a lighter?" she asked. I didn't, of course, but Elna went digging in her purse. While she searched, I looked at the lady's face. She was probably thirty. She was missing a tooth. Her hair was long and sectioned into two yellow braids, secured with different-colored rubber bands. While I looked at the lady, the lady looked at Elna, who, after a few moments of scrounging, produced a lighter and held it out before her. The lady didn't take it, though. She took a sudden step back, surveying Elna with a wary eye.

"There's something very dark in you," she said, after a pause. Her manner was plain and steady. Unemotional. Like she was pointing out an exit on the highway, or an unusual cloud on the horizon. She said this, and then she gathered up her bag of found cigarettes and hobbled off around the corner. Elna looked taken aback. I hadn't seen her quite that way before. Not even by the lake on Christmas Eve.

"Crazy bitch," she said, tucking the lighter back into her purse. The words were hard and cold, but her voice wasn't. It wavered. "Let's go find someplace to stay," she muttered.

21

By the time we got to the motel, it was nearly midnight. Elna parked far off to the side, behind a large dumpster, concealing the car from view. The lot was mostly empty. An old woman leaned out a second-floor window, picking at her scalp, a bedsheet draped around her shoulders like a cape. The smell of hot laundry wafted out from the basement vents as we made our way around to the front entrance. It reminded me of Mineral, of my home in the store, of going down to our own laundry to collect the coins. As I thought about it, I could almost hear them clanging around as I sorted them into their rolls. Green for dimes. Yellow for pennies. Red, blue, quarters, nickels. The paper rolls had a particular smell. Like pencil shavings and Easter egg dye. I liked the weight of them in my palm. I liked carrying them to the bank each Sunday. Then I remembered that it was Saturday, and that tomorrow would be Sunday, and I wondered if anyone was going to bring the coins to the bank or if they were just building up in the machines. Probably, neither Jen nor my mother had this on their minds. They were probably worried sick. I could imagine them sitting at the table together, gray in the face. I felt bad, but right beneath the bad was a flicker of anger at having been lied to for so long.

Inside, the desk attendant eyed us carefully. His gaze lingered on Elna for a few seconds, surveying her body for a slow moment before saying, "Checking in?"

"One room, just overnight please." She dug around in her purse for her wallet.

The man turned to me and said, "How old are you?"

"She's sixteen," Elna interjected, taking a step forward and leaning her elbows down on the desk. I looked at her smiling profile, the shine of her canine teeth glinting under the overhead lights. These made a noise like the ones at my school did. All fluorescent lights seemed to. I wished I could shut off every light in the world. "I take care of her," she continued, nudging her head in my direction. "We're on our way home." The man stared at us.

"I'm eighteen," she added.

"Is that so?"

"It is," she cooed.

"Where you girls coming from?"

"Portland."

The man nodded. "Where's home?" he asked.

"Carson City," Elna responded, not missing a beat. I could picture the shape of Nevada in my mind, Carson City marked with a little red star in the left corner, just barely over the California border. "We're really very tired," she continued. "We've had such a long drive just to get here. And my sister, she needs to take her medicine and rest."

"You sick?" he asked me.

"My heart is bad," I whispered, lifting my hand to my chest and resting it gently over the breastbone, surprised by how quickly this half lie came to me. He nodded seriously, looking over a paper ledger with different numbers written on it. Within a few minutes, we had a key to a room, and Elna had given him some cash. We walked down a long corridor with thick green carpeting. The walls had pictures of old famous people in yellowing frames. People who'd certainly never been here, to this motel. Had surely never even been to Eureka at all. I recognized some of their faces. One of the pictures was turned upside down, just hanging on its nail with Rita Hayworth's smiling face flipped toward the ceiling. I wondered if it was put up like that in the first place, or if it fell and someone nailed it back in without noticing. Everything smelled damp.

The room had two twin beds on either side of a dinged-up nightstand. There was a lamp with a torn orange shade. A TV bolted down to the top of the dresser. A closet with a floral fabric–covered ironing board and rust on the legs. I went to look around the bathroom and saw that the faucet let out a continual stream of water. Just barely more than a drip. The door saddle squeaked when I stepped on it going back into the main room. Elna was sitting on the bed near the window, looking out onto the parking lot, her posture hunched. She seemed very young to me, suddenly. Like any other kid. She turned around and met my gaze, like she could feel I was looking at her. There were soft, purple shadows beneath her eyes. The polish on a few of her fingers had chipped off completely and I could see the pale shells of her nails on her tiny, freckled hands. It was harder not to think about everything here in the quiet box of a motel room. In the car, at least, there was movement and sound, fast-changing scenery and signs to pay attention to. There was a map to look at. A line I could trace from Mineral to San Francisco, tracking our progress as the hours ticked by. On the street earlier, there was the distraction of a cheeseburger. Wedding gowns. People going about their lives.

Now, I didn't know what to do with myself. I went over to the bed nearer to the doorway and opened up my bag. Unpacking felt pointless. I imagined taking out the few pieces of clothing I'd brought and laying them in the rickety dresser, shutting the drawer, and then retrieving them again in the morning. The idea of it made me sad and nervous. I zipped the bag and looked at the wall, hoping something would suddenly just make sense.

As if she could feel my need for a task, Elna said, "I think I left my little backpack with all my makeup in the car. It must still be in the trunk." She dug the keys from her back pocket and tossed them on my bed. "Would you go out there and get it for me?" she asked, looking down at her nails. I told her I would. I was relieved to have a reason to get out of the room.

The air out in the parking lot was heavy with mist. Fog hung over the tops of the trees and the streetlamps, illuminated from below by the yellow lights dotting the motel's property. We weren't far from the ocean. Maybe a fifteen-minute drive. The bones under my skin felt heavy. My whole body felt like a big, awkward puppet that I was operating from inside a little control room somewhere in my brain. It felt like that often, but on this night, it was especially intense. It was like the puppet was in need of many repairs but had no chance of getting them anytime soon. Stiff, creaky joints begging for oil. A total failure of mechanics behind the face.

I made it to the car and opened the trunk, slinging Elna's bag over one shoulder and locking the car again. Even though I was not aware of anyone watching me, I behaved as though many people were. I tossed my hair back over one shoulder like a girl in a shampoo commercial. I pretended this was my own car, that I was nineteen and not fourteen, that this fashionable miniature backpack was something I'd bought for myself in a shopping mall, with money I'd made at my own job, and that I was on a road trip I really wanted to be on, something planned, something ending in a place where I would be welcomed and expected. As I walked, I dug a lip gloss out of the backpack and smeared the wand across my mouth. It smelled like cotton candy. The gloss had a grainy texture. Particles of lavender glitter found their way between my teeth.

Then, maybe fifteen feet from the lobby entrance, I stopped. A heavy sadness had come over me suddenly, like a hand lurching out from behind and grabbing me by the neck before I could walk any farther. The air felt colder. I didn't want to go back inside. I didn't want to go home, to Mineral, either, or even to San Francisco. A lump grew in my throat. I wanted to be someplace else, badly, but couldn't say where. I'd had that feeling all my life. This homesickness for somewhere I'd never been. Like I was always longing to go back to a place I couldn't even picture. Nowhere I could find on any map. I wasn't even sure it really existed. Something told me I'd be looking for it until I died.

I could remember being a kid in the store with my mother, the only woman I'd ever known as my mother, sitting on a stool behind the counter with her while she balanced the books. Bright, gray light pouring in through the front window. A cold draft creeping under the door. I'd felt an aching in my gut, that same invisible hand reaching out.

"I want to go home," I'd said.

"You are home," she replied, distractedly.

"No, I want to go *home,*" I repeated. We went back and forth like this, me trying and failing to explain myself again and again, and she insisting I was home already, growing more agitated and exasperated as we went on. She seemed offended, I could tell, but beneath that there seemed to be a deep pool of worry. I didn't say it to her anymore after that, but I thought it all the time.

That same feeling was with me now, so sharp my eyes began to water. I looked up at the sky and wished a funnel of light would come down, pass through the fog, and beam me up into the quiet vacuum of space. If a rocket full of aliens landed in the parking lot right then, I would've hopped right in, no question. I wiped my eyes, then tried to focus my gaze on the bark of the tree that grew in the curb planter in front of me. I tried to follow the patterns in the wood, find shapes in the grain. A rabbit, an apple, a baby's round face. I leaned closer to the tree, squinting against the dim light. I ran my fingers over the bark.

Then, I heard a voice behind me call, "Are you okay?" It was a woman. She sounded middle-aged. I wondered how long I'd been standing there. Goosebumps spread along my arms. "Young lady?" the voice said.

I forced the puppet of my body to turn around and face the stranger. She had a wrinkly, worried expression. Big, curly hair and bright orange lipstick. She kept a reasonable distance from me. I noticed her hand stayed firmly on the strap of her purse. "Are you okay?" she repeated. I nodded, though she didn't seem convinced because she then asked if I wanted her to call some-one.

"Who?" I replied, genuinely curious. The motel's neon sign buzzed loudly above the entrance. The woman looked around. I could tell she wasn't sure what to do. It was cold and clammy outside, and she was clearly on her way to her car, keys in hand. A discount card for a grocery chain dangled off the ring. There was a rhinestone-heart bobble, and a little Swiss Army knife folded up into a compact rectangle no bigger than her thumb.

"Are you in need of any kind of help?" Her words came out slowly. A deliberate little pause between each one. I clenched my teeth. Her voice had changed now. I recognized the tone immediately. She really thought something was the matter with me. Nothing I could do would change her mind about that now. Some of the apprehension and concern in her voice had turned to a kind of pitying condescension. I shook my head no.

"Are you sure?" she pressed, tone unchanged. A terrible, unscratchable itch crept down my back. I wanted the woman to be quiet. I wanted her to get as far away from me as possible. I could see the pores in her cheeks, shadowy little craters under the harsh lamplight. Her lipstick bled out into the faint cracks in the skin around her wide, fleshy mouth. I could smell the faint, florid powder of her hair spray drifting over to me. She pushed her eyebrows together, frowning. The itch grew stronger. It started to burn. It spread into my brain. Every thought that passed through me seemed engulfed in a furious, raging blaze. My mouth felt hot. My tongue felt hot. The whites of my eyes felt hot.

I was so tired of people talking to me with that voice and looking at me with that same kind of expression on their face. I was so tired of people thinking I needed help, and trying to give it to me whether I asked for it or not, and the way I could tell they felt so certain they knew what was best for me, even when they didn't know me at all. I didn't want this woman, a stranger, to call anyone. I didn't want her to look at me anymore. I didn't care if her intentions were good, I didn't care if she had a daughter my age, or if she could see I had no business being alone out there in the parking lot of the Driftwood Roadhouse late at night. I knew there were a lot of things I needed. I knew I wasn't supposed to be out in some cold, sodden part of California with ancient trees and sad, desolate beaches and people who were all strangers while people at home, the people who knew me, were probably sick to their stomachs, searching. I knew I needed help. It's just that I didn't believe there was anyone in this world who could really give it to me.

"I don't need anything from you," I told the woman.

22

Later that night, Elna and I went down to the swimming pool. It was on the other side of the check-in area, behind a yellowed glass door with a big sign on it that said *No lifeguard on duty.* By the time we went down there, the front desk was unattended. We found the door left ajar, and the pool empty.

We took our clothes off and tossed them on a folding chair, then stood at the edge of the water in our underwear, with a couple of thin, rough towels draped around our necks. The air in the pool room was steamy, and heavy with blue-smelling chemicals. My eyes began to burn around the edges. There was a big, tile mosaic of a castle on the far wall. It was sort of clumsy-looking, with some of the tiles too large and others too small, and some sections having so many missing tiles I could see the Sheetrock behind it. Beneath the castle, a grimy diving board was positioned in the center of the deep end.

Elna knelt down and slid into the pool like a snake, her body slipping beneath the surface in one fast, quiet motion. She bobbed up, then dipped her head under and flipped it back, smoothing her hair down. Beads of water rolled down her face.

"I thought you liked to dive?" she asked, floating in place a few feet from where I stood, her arms treading gentle circles. She still had her jewelry on, sparkly stars on her earlobes and a necklace with a shiny, purple butterfly charm.

"I do," I said. But I'd only ever done it at Needle Lake. Never in a pool. Before this night, I hadn't actually seen a pool in real life. Only in movies. And now, after everything, the idea of doing it at all gave me a sick, cold feeling. I wrapped the towel tighter around my shoulders but it didn't help.

She stared at me, empty-eyed, before saying, "You told me you were into diving."

"Yeah," I answered.

"So," she said, pointing to the other end of the pool, "dive." I hesitated, looking from one end to the other. Goosebumps spread over my legs.

"Dive," she repeated, staring at me. Her voice was firm.

My heart fluttered as I walked to the edge of the board, then stood on it. Elna's gaze was fixed on me in a way that made it feel like she could see down into the middle of my bones. Her telling me to dive felt more like a dare than a command. If I didn't do it, I thought, I'd be ruining something. Whatever trust she had in me, maybe, to stay quiet about the lake, to follow her lead. To go along with her all the way to San Francisco. I didn't want her to think differently of me. I didn't want to mess things up. But mostly, I still wanted her to like me.

I looked down into the water. I knew it was the same as any other water—a lake, an ocean, a bathtub. Water was water and I would float in any of it just the same. But still, my stomach flipped over on itself and the skin on the back of my neck felt hot and prickly. I pushed my weight down on the board and felt it move. I'd only ever leapt into the water from the dock, solid and familiar. I hated the way this new thing wobbled beneath me, bouncing me up and down as I moved closer to the edge.

In my mind, I tried to go back to the place I knew. I pictured the trail up to the lake in the early morning light, moss glowing green in the shelter of the silent forest and the soft give of earth under my feet. I imagined emerging from the tree cover out over the mountaintop, seeing the sun gleaming over the lake's still surface. But then, when I saw myself drawing near the water, near enough to see my reflection, I saw Tom. Stiff and blue-lipped. I imagined myself diving past him, forcing myself to plunge beneath the surface, down toward the lake bed, a place I'd always known to be still and silent, dotted with strange, forgotten treasures. But he was there, too. Bobbing around the silt. Staring at me with wide, dead eyes. Limbs bloated and pale. Fish feeding on his toes.

I thought I might vomit. I took a hard swallow to stop it, and forced myself to jump from the board then, taking a couple pushes down with my feet to give some momentum, the way I'd seen done in movies. The castle mosaic flashed over my eyes in a blur, then the yellowy overhead lights with all the dead bugs trapped under the plastic fixtures. Then, Elna, now crouching at the side of the pool, watching. Then, the water.

Once I was under, it didn't really feel different than the lake as I knew it. Just for a moment, I found that quiet, sunken peace. Every thought vanished from my mind. A cool, merciful hand wiped away the film of anxiety and dread, like clearing fog from a mirror. A brief moment of clarity before everything was murky again. I wanted so badly to just stay there. Spend my life in the hushed underlayer. If I were given three wishes, I'd be transformed into a fish. A buffalo fish, because they could live in lakes for more than a hundred years and weren't prized by anglers. I wouldn't even need the other two wishes, if I could have this. I'd give them away to other people. I was told by my mother I'd always been drawn to water. She liked to tell again and again the story of me as a toddler, brought to Ruby Beach in Olympic, running straight into the rough, cold surf when no one was looking.

I bobbed up to the pool's surface and took a gulp of air. Elna beckoned to me, and I paddled over to the side where she sat. I was about to ask her if she was going to dive, too, but then without warning she placed her hand firmly on top of my head and pushed me back underwater. She gripped my hair with her fingers and held it tightly. I could feel her knuckles digging into my scalp, tipping me back so that my face turned upward. For the first moment, I was confused. I didn't know what to make of it. I opened my eyes, forcing myself to think past the sting of the chlorine. I could see her blurry figure looming above the surface, up in the open air. She seemed to be looking straight down at me.

I tried to push my way up, but found her grip impossible to break free of. I reached toward the ledge, batting at where I thought her legs were, but she just stayed there, holding my head in place. Normally, I could hold my breath for a long time. One hundred and one seconds, at my record. But this wasn't like that at all. Everything I knew about keeping air in my lungs, letting it out slowly in ribbons of quiet bubbles, staying calm and still, left me. I felt a surge of panic blow through my body. A strange throbbing in my chest.

And then, I saw it all from the edge of the pool, somehow. As if I were sitting up there with my legs dangling in the water, as if I were some stranger, a guest of the motel, observing it all from the sidelines. I saw myself reaching out toward the water, offering a hand, and I tried to bring my body toward that fragment of myself but found that I just couldn't get there.

One moment I was under, flailing and kicking, and the next my face had emerged back into the air and my mouth was open, gasping, my hair plastered over my eyes. Stale, bitter-tasting water ran down my throat and gathered in my ears. Once I'd gotten some breath into my lungs, my vision started to clear. The room un-tilted itself. The first sensation to return to me was the feeling of my fingers grazing the rough spackling of the pool walls. I saw the castle mosaic. I saw our clothes piled on the other side of the room.

And then I saw Elna. She stood up, lazily stretched her arms out, and then hopped into the water in a carefree, childlike plunk. I felt an urge to leave the pool then, but my body felt stunned and exhausted. All I could manage was to stay there at the side, hanging on to the ledge. She dipped under and then popped back up, treading water just a couple feet away from me. The waves from her jump lapped at my chin. She was smiling, the reflection of her face spreading in wild ripples out before her. She watched me as I pushed all the hair back from my face. I could see her searching my expression, waiting for me to give some kind of reaction. I just stayed in place, trying to catch my breath, heart racing and twinging with little flashes of that strange, empty ache. I didn't know what I could say. If I should say anything at all, even. Like maybe it was better to pretend nothing had happened. I thought about tomorrow when we'd start our last drive to San Francisco. I estimated we had about seven hours left. Finally, Elna splashed a little water my way. It got in my eyes and stung.

She said to me, "Don't be upset. I was just playing around."

23

Elna fell asleep almost instantly that night when we got back to the room. I could smell the pool chemicals drifting off her damp hair, filling the air as she turned her head on the pillow. I didn't feel like I could sleep. I couldn't even bring myself to lie down on the bed next to her. I just stood there in the dark, arms at my sides, watching. The room was completely black except for a thin sliver of light beaming in from the streetlamp in the parking lot, just between where the curtains met. It fell across her neck, casting the contours of her face in a dim, bluish glow. I stood still and quiet for so long I lost any sense of time. My feet began to feel like they were a part of the carpet. My arms felt first like dead, empty weight, and then gradually began to feel like nothing at all.

Eventually, a car alarm went off in the lot below the window and Elna stirred, flipping herself to the side and pulling the pillow over her head. The sound jerked me back into my body, and I took the spare blanket from the closet then, bringing it into the unlit bathroom, where I wrapped it around me as tightly as I could. I brought the top all the way up to my eyes and turned against the wall a few times, squeezing the air out and compressing myself inside the fabric. Then I lay down on the tile floor, rolling to position myself beneath the sink cabinet. It was only about a foot off the ground, and not quite as long as I was tall.

I would sometimes fall asleep like this, mummified in bedding, wedged into strange places, at home in Mineral. My mother had once discovered me zipped inside a sleeping bag beneath my bed. Once, beneath my actual mattress. I'd squeezed myself under it on a sudden urge, and even though I could barely lift it back up enough to get out, the heaviness against my body soothed me so intensely I drifted off. When I woke up, my legs were numb but I felt better than I had in days. The last time I could remember doing it was after the bus incident, when my mother found me on the floor of my closet, hidden beneath a stack of quilts, in a deep sleep. She asked if anything was wrong, and I told her no, sliding the door shut again to make it dark. I knew she stood there for a few more minutes, because I could hear her breathing, but soon she turned and left without another comment.

There in the bathroom of the motel, I listened to the sound of my breathing. I listened to the watery rumblings of pipes inside the wall, the vague murmur of a TV in another room. When my thoughts turned to what had just happened downstairs in the pool, I reached into my head and pushed them away. I tried to think instead about my geography bee materials. I'd brought some of them with me in my bag. I didn't want to unfurl myself from the blanket to go retrieve them. Instead, staring out into the dark, I moved each card from my mind into the open air, trying to hold them there, studying them one by one, like projector slides only I could see. It worked for a little while. My brain felt lighter. I didn't feel so conscious of having a damp, pulsing body covered in millions of itchy hairs. I thought only about the sprawl of lines on tiny maps. The order of colors on floating, ghostly flags. Symbols, stripes, the exact width of borders.

When I got to Palau, I conjured first the brilliant blue background. I could see it so clear, so bright, my eyes nearly burned. Blue like the sky reflected in the surface of the sea. Blue like the sparkling, shallow ocean nearing the shoreline in a faraway place. But then, like a wave of sudden nausea seizing my gut, there came the blue of the pool, cloying and artificial. The stinging in my throat. The wobbling glare of the overhead lights as I looked to the surface. My heart began to race. I pushed it all away with every ounce of strength I had, squeezing my eyes shut until tears began to form in the crease between my lids. I held my breath. I waited.

And then I got back to the order of things. Tracing the shape of the sun, just left of center against the turquoise background. Filling it in with its particular shade of yellow. I'd drawn the flag of Palau lots of times in the margins of my papers at school. I had three colored pencils which, if layered all together, resulted in a near-perfect imitation of the miniature flag from the embassy. Buttercup, daffodil, goldenrod. I could picture the waxy sheen they left on the surface of the paper, the smooth curl of their shavings falling into the basket, barely making a sound, as I twisted them through the wall sharpener. The tin box the pencils rested in, all laid in a rainbow in their individual grooves. How perfectly it fit in the front pocket of my backpack. The way the box looked lined up with all my other stationery supplies on my desk at home. My desk with all its neat piles of paper maps and drawer full of composition notebooks with the black-and-white-speckled covers. My chair with the worn green cushion. My lamp with the bumblebee charm pull-chain.

And then, before I knew it, all I was thinking about was home. I didn't feel that same wave of sick panic this time like I did when the pool water came back to me. Instead, there came a heavy sadness. Dragging and scratchy. Like a soaking-wet wool coat that could not be taken off my body. I tried to get out from inside of it but found myself trapped, collapsing beneath its weight.

I found myself thinking about one early morning last summer. School had been out for a couple weeks and my nerves had finally calmed to the point where I didn't feel sick every day. I remember waking up to the sound of mourning doves gently cooing in the yard. A soft beam of yellow sunlight peeked in through the window by my bed and diffused over the quilt and the carpet. Warm, sweet-smelling air drifted beneath the door. Cut grass and berries, ripened by the heat of the day. I remember looking out my window and seeing Jen standing on a thick, low-slung branch of our gnarled old bigleaf maple tree in the corner of the backyard. She was holding a long silver pipe in her hands, pointing it down toward the ground and gazing through it. I went outside in my cotton pajamas, rolling up the ankles to keep my hems from the morning dew.

"Look," Jen said, pulling a little stack of circular magnets from her pocket. I stood on the branch next to her, the bark soft and mossy beneath my bare feet. She dropped the magnets in and had me look straight down the tube. I watched as they spun lazily and fell, slowly, as if through molasses, before eventually dropping out the bottom end and meeting the grass with a soft thud. I picked the magnets up and examined them, puzzled. "My brother showed me this once when I was a kid," Jen said. "I don't know what made me think of it this morning, but I thought you'd like it." We watched the magnets move through the pipe with the same strange, suspended motion again and again. "It's this thing called Lenz's law," she explained, her voice quiet with awe. "You need an aluminum or a copper tube. I just had this extra piece in the back of my truck." She went on to tell me about how after being dropped in, the magnets caused the surrounding metal to produce an electrical current with its own field strong enough to oppose their motion. "There's a little fight against gravity going on in there," she said.

When I looked out into the dark of the bathroom, all I could see was the two of us standing together beneath that tree, surrounded by its wealth of marvelously large green leaves, watching one of the universe's many simple and elegant magic tricks unfolding before our eyes. I tried to hold the image there, to keep myself in the memory before it could turn to mist.

. . .

I must have fallen asleep, because the next thing I saw was Elna standing in the doorway, daylight beaming in from behind the outline of her body. She had her boots on already. That blue-chemical smell still hung heavy in the air. She flipped the light on and stared at me under the sink, her gaze traveling the length of the cocooned blanket.

She raised one brow, but only said, "Come on. We need to get on the road. If we leave now, we'll get to San Francisco around dusk."

24

By the time we pulled onto the Golden Gate Bridge, the sky had turned a faded pink and the sun was dipping near the horizon. I could see streaks of purple light glowing through the clouds, a thick layer of fog hovering over the water below. It reached all the way up to the cables, wisps of vapor trailing the brake lights on the cars ahead of us. There was a big, cheerful color photo of this bridge on the table of contents page in my social studies textbook at school. I'd looked at it many times, studying the way it seemed to rise from the mist, the arches appearing truly golden, almost on fire, in the brilliant morning. I thought it looked impressive. I wondered if I'd ever see it in person.

Being on it now, I was impressed. It was bigger than I could've imagined from the picture, even higher in the air than I'd realized. But it didn't feel cheerful. There was something almost forbidding about it, instead. Gloomy and strange, like a passage into another world. Traffic slowed to a standstill, and I looked around at all the people in the surrounding cars, each of them wrapped up in their own thoughts, on their way to places unknown to me, just moments from disappearing from my view forever. I saw a bright yellow telephone bolted to the guardrail with a sign over it that read *THERE IS HOPE.* Beyond the edge, heavy fog that seemed to go on forever.

I looked over at Elna. When we'd gotten in the car that morning, she'd put the radio on and said nothing about what happened the night before. She'd seemed her usual self, a little blithe and aloof underneath the layers of charm, chatting about different things, adjusting her hair in the rearview occasionally. Then, maybe an hour or so from the city, a grim feeling started to gather around her. I noticed her mouth tighten, her jaw set like she was clenching her teeth. She grew very quiet. By the time the skyline was in view, she'd turned the music off and wasn't speaking at all. Her skin even seemed to change color. Just slightly, barely perceptible in the waning daylight, but I could see that she looked paler. Grayish, almost.

The traffic dissipated, and she sighed, cracking her neck as she switched her steering hand. I faced forward, watching the buildings grow larger on the horizon. Hundreds upon hundreds spilling out toward the waterline, little dots of light in the windows. I was amazed by the sprawl of it all, by how many people it must have contained, by the way it seemed to almost appear suddenly, like a mirage, after days of driving past desolate coasts and little forest towns, half deserted.

When we pulled off the bridge, I asked Elna, "How much farther?"

"We're not far," she said. "But I have to make a quick stop first."

"Where?"

"I just want to get these off my hands before we're back at Candace's." She shook her coat pocket and I heard the sound of pills rattling against each other. I realized they must have been what was left of what we'd taken from Tom, the bottle she slipped into my jacket while we were in his apartment. I didn't even know she'd grabbed them out of my room before we left Mineral. I nodded, though a knot had begun to form in my stomach. Nothing was familiar. Not the buildings, now towering stories above the car, or the street signs with names I'd never seen, or the bustle of many strange faces all blurring into one another as groups of laughing, shouting people shouldered past one another on the sidewalks. We drove deeper into the city, swirling neon lights leaving trails in my vision. I cracked the window and breathed in the traces of hot dogs and caramel corn from rolling carts, gasoline, cigarette smoke, sewage.

After maybe fifteen minutes, Elna turned off the avenue. The corner post read, *TURK STREET.* Cars kept whizzing by behind us on the main drag, but no others followed down here. It was quiet. Few people on the sidewalks. By now, the sun had left the sky and the streetlights started to blink on, their beams casting everything in a dim, yellow haze.

Elna parallel-parked easily, barely having to look back over her shoulder, outside a place called the Page Hotel. It was much shorter than the buildings I'd seen coming in off the bridge, dirty beige brick with tiny square windows and a rusty fire escape.

"Wait here," she said. "And keep the car locked while I'm in there." I watched as she slid out of the driver's seat and walked around the front, stepping nimbly over the curb and approaching the entrance. The door to the hotel was enclosed behind a wrought iron gate. It looked old, with elaborate curls and spires rising high above where anyone could climb. She pressed a button on an intercom. I heard a crackling static and then a high-pitched buzzing noise before she disappeared inside. I sat there, wringing my fingers in nervous twists. I didn't like waiting in this place. I didn't like the look of the hotel, or the way the wind was blowing loose trash across the street. I didn't like that I had no idea where we were, exactly, on the map, and even if I had the energy to look at the one in the glove box, it wouldn't show me the city in any detail, wouldn't help me to understand how close we were to Candace's apartment. I realized then that I didn't even know her address, and I didn't like that either.

There was a thin man sitting on the sidewalk near the iron gate, a dirty blanket draped like a cloak over his shoulders and head. He was shivering so hard his eyes looked blurry. Lots of small objects were arranged around him in a half circle. A silver fork, a cassette player with a piece of tape on the front that said *KAITLYN,* one cookie jar with a cat on the lid and another in the shape of a hot-air balloon. There was a half-deflated basketball next to three pairs of glasses, all lined up in a row. He reached out and touched these things every few moments, just laying his hand gently atop them one by one before crossing his arms back over his middle.

I looked at the clock in the console. Only five minutes had passed. It already felt like an hour. I took a deep breath. I told myself she'd be out in another five minutes. Then, I thought, what if she wasn't? What if she didn't come back out again at all? My heart began to race a little.

I heard the gate creak open and turned around to look. It wasn't Elna. It was a girl about my age in a halter top and snakeskin-print miniskirt. I watched as she looked both ways down the sidewalk before sprinting across the street. She passed in front of the windshield, and we made eye contact for a quick moment as she dashed. Her eyelashes were very long. There was a scabbed cut on one of her cheeks. Within seconds, she disappeared inside another building.

I stared down at the floorboard and thought about what I would be doing if I hadn't left home. I'd be in my room, maybe, sorting through my maps. The store would be open for another hour or two. If someone came in, the bells on the door would chime softly and I would hear it, muffled, from my desk. Maybe something would be cooking in the oven, and I'd catch the smell of it wafting down the hall. I could conjure it all so clearly. The way the floorboards in my room felt so smooth and familiar on the soles of my feet. How I knew exactly where the creaks were. How it sounded when the wind rustled loose leaves against my window.

The thought of the store, of home, seemed so wonderful to me then. I was taken aback by my own longing, the suddenness and intensity of it. It felt like standing on a dark ridge in a strange, vast forest and spotting a little fire glowing in the distance, warm and bright, and wanting so badly to lie down alongside it, feel its heat against my face, but knowing I couldn't find my way there. My eyes began to sting. A tear gathered, wobbling on my lower lid before rolling down my face and falling onto my lap.

When I looked up, Elna was on her way back toward the car.

25

The front door to Candace's apartment opened into a little vestibule full of sweet-smelling smoke. Little cones of incense burned orange against the low light. I noticed a tall stack of unopened mail on a wobbly-looking side table and a mountain of shoes piled in the corner. High-heeled sandals, feathered slippers. A single man's construction boot, unlaced. Colorful, plastic beads hung from a ceiling fan which dangled half loose, wires poking out from where the plaster met the base. I followed Elna inside, staying close behind her. Once I got past the doorframe, I detected something fetid beneath the sweet incense. Something vague and lingering, like a piece of meat left out in the sun. There was a crusty, plastic fork on the ground. Elna kicked it out of the way and turned to me quickly, holding up one finger for me to wait a minute, then turned the corner into the main room. I peeked around the side after her, just barely enough to see in.

There was Candace, reclined against many pillows on a green velvet sofa, reading a magazine. Her hair was lighter now. Dyed platinum blond and swirled up into a wispy bun at the top of her head. She wore false eyelashes. Her skin had a grayish tint, especially beneath the eyes. She was still pretty, like I remembered, but she looked like she'd been sick for a long time. I stayed back, my view partially obscured by Elna's shoulder.

"I tried calling," Elna said.

"Oh?" Candace replied, without glancing up. "I didn't hear the phone ring."

"How was the place?"

"Great." She picked up a bottle of store-brand pink lemonade from the floor and took a big sip, still not looking up from the magazine. She ripped out a perfume sample packet and held it to her nose, inhaling deeply. "I'm feeling really good now," she said.

"Yeah?"

"Did they call you and tell you I was getting sent home?"

"No. I called them." Elna's voice was tight.

"Did you bring any groceries?"

"What?" Elna asked.

"Groceries," Candace repeated, putting the magazine down. "Everything in the fridge rotted while I was gone."

"I've been driving for two days," she said, setting our bags down hard at her side. "So, no. I didn't."

"Well." Candace sighed.

"Look," Elna said, reaching back around the corner and yanking me by the shoulder. I stumbled into the room. She pushed me in front of her. "Look what I brought back."

Candace blinked at me for a few seconds, then lifted her arms out and broke into a loose, wet smile. "I can't believe it," she said. "My girl. Are you real?" Elna gave me a little shove in the lower back, sending me stumbling toward the sofa. "Are you really real?" she asked again.

"I'm real," I said.

"I know you are," she cooed, winking an eye. "What an amazing thing. Come here." She patted the cushion beside her. My eyes fell on the coffee table. An assortment of translucent, orange pill bottles lay scattered across a tray. I could read the tiny print from where I stood. Her first and last name under the marquee of several different pharmacies. There were a couple lit candles flickering around the tray. She kept saying *My girl, my girl* over and over, shaking her head, her frothy pile of hair wobbling from side to side. I went over and sat on a chair opposite the couch, facing her. I could see Elna looking angrily from the coffee table to Candace. Her eyes were dark and shining.

"I need to wash my hair," she clipped, walking down the hall and around a corner, dragging one of her bags behind her.

Candace stared after her, looking a little dazed and annoyed, before standing up and hobbling over to me. I felt frozen in place. It must have taken her only a couple of seconds to get to the other side of the table but watching her draw nearer, time seemed to stretch into a long, thin rope. The moment warped and flattened, spinning out like wet clay. I felt even then like I would always recall it sharply. Like it was a moment I would never really get out of, no matter how many days passed. She pressed her hands to either side of my face. Her fingers were cool and smooth, nails painted purple and filed into slender ovals, like Elna's. She wore many rings.

"Hi, baby," she whispered. I could feel her breath against my skin. Her mouth smelled sweet and a little rotten.

"Hi," I said.

"I can't believe you're here."

"Me neither."

"Does my sister know you're here?"

"Yes," I lied.

"Good, good." She shuffled back to the couch. I stayed in the chair, legs crossed in a stiff, almost formal posture. I felt so intensely aware of my body I almost couldn't stand it. I had a strong urge to hit myself in the face, just to jolt myself into a different feeling, but discreetly tucked my hand under my thigh so I wouldn't. Back in her spot on the couch, surrounded by throw pillows, Candace smiled at me. She picked up the jug of lemonade again and took a long drink. I watched as her gullet moved up and down. A drip rolled steadily from her chin down her chest. She tipped the jug toward me, and I shook my head no.

Then, I heard myself say, "Is what Elna told me true?"

She just smiled wider. A long minute passed. "You're my baby, if that's what you mean," she finally said.

I looked all around the room again. There was a movie poster taped up in the corner. Three women in denim short-shorts, blood-splattered, running from a man in a cheap-looking rubber mask. One of them, unmistakably, Candace.

"You were in that movie?" I asked, badly wanting a quick escape from the moment. It all felt like too much. Unbearably intense, too bright to stare straight into, even though there was a part of me that couldn't stand to look away.

"About a million years ago," she said.

"What was it about?" I half listened as she told me the plot. Something about three girls moving into a haunted dormitory for summer school. Her character getting lost in the storage room in her nightgown, the killer lunging out of a refrigerator box. Suddenly, I burst out, "Why did you give me away?" My voice came out a little too loudly. I gripped the sides of the chair tightly.

Candace let out a ragged sigh. "First of all," she said, "Anne really wanted you. You have to know that." She looked at me seriously, her eyes locking with mine. "And my sister was just desperate for a baby, but how was she going to get pregnant? She wasn't the type to just suck it up and find some guy at a bar. Which is what I would've done, by the way." She raised an eyebrow and wagged a finger at me, as if this were advice I would want, maybe even need, someday. "I mean, ten minutes in the car and then done. Baby on the way. What's the big deal? But you know, that's Anne. And of course, an unmarried woman wasn't going to be allowed to adopt. Especially back then. So, it just worked out." She shrugged, taking another drink of lemonade.

As she drank, my eyes fell on her feet. They were resting on the end of the sofa, one atop the other. Her toenails were painted lime green. She had a little golden ring with a heart emblem on the second right toe. I noticed how narrow and knobby they were, with the third one in on each foot noticeably longer than the others. Nearly invisible little toenails. Sharp ankles. High arches. They looked so much like my own I felt dizzy. She picked up one of the open pill bottles, shook a few into her palm, and swallowed them down.

"And I wasn't in a great place back then," she continued. "It was hard having just one kid. And expensive. I was losing my mind. You were a good baby, though. Don't think you weren't. I mean, you were the quietest baby I'd ever met. Hardly ever cried. Never screamed. Elna wasn't like that at all." Candace rolled her eyes and pushed a piece of hair from her forehead. "She was such a terror. I used to joke with her that I should've kept you and sent her up to Washington." I could hear the shower running from down the hall, the sound of Elna pulling back the plastic curtain and adjusting the faucet. "But anyway," Candace went on. "I would always tell Anne how hard of a time I was having and finally one day she told me to just bring you up to her so I could have a break. What a relief that was. It wasn't supposed to be permanent, at first. But I think we both knew pretty quickly that it was for the best."

"Elna said you almost came back to get me."

"I thought about it. I did come close, once or twice. I'm sure my sister was always a little scared that I would. We didn't do any paperwork or anything, so nobody could've stopped me."

I slid both my hands under my legs and leaned forward, pressing the full weight of my body down onto them. I shut my eyes. It would have been so easy for everything to be completely different, I thought. All those years, any day, I could've been whisked away from my life. I might've never met Jen. I might've never discovered diving. I realized then how glad I was that Candace never came up to Mineral to bring me back to this cluttered, dirty place, but that realization came with a strange, sad pang of guilt I didn't quite know how to understand. I squeezed my eyes shut harder, trying to flatten all my feelings down.

Candace leaned over and squeezed my knee. I wished she wouldn't, but I could tell she meant it in a sympathetic way, so I didn't say anything. After a moment, she released her grip and returned to her position on the sofa. I opened my eyes and the room looked tilted, like someone had reached their hand down from above and just shifted the whole world slightly off-center. I looked around at the apartment and thought more about how easily it could have been home for me. If she'd changed her mind before bringing me to Washington in the first place, if she came back after just a week or two. I felt like I'd been dropped into the periphery of an alternate timeline, where I could see all the ghosts of a life that nearly came true. There was a sour taste in the back of my mouth.

"You only ever came to visit that one time," I said.

"For your birthday, I remember. First day of February."

"Why?"

"Well, it's a long drive, for one thing." Candace sighed.

"I know," I said, a little annoyed. "I just did it."

"And it was tough on me, too. I mean, I felt pretty weird after leaving that visit." Her voice cracked a little on *leaving.* She shook another pill loose from one of the bottles and swallowed it dry.

"I don't understand why nobody ever told me this," I said.

"Anne and I discussed it a few times. I said I had no problem with the idea, but she was never sure. Personally, I think she couldn't get up the nerve. She was always coming up with different reasons to put it off."

"Elna thinks she was hoping I'd find out during her stay with us. So she wouldn't have to explain it herself."

"Yeah, that sounds like Anne." Candace rolled her eyes. "It really was for the best though, Ida," she added, her voice now soft and quiet. "I never told my sister this back then, but I guess there's no harm in telling you now that you're nearly grown already. I was getting pretty worried about Elna around you. She was so upset about having a baby in the house. Very jealous." Candace sighed and chuckled a little. As the chuckle faded, her mouth flattened into a grimace. There were so many little parts of different expressions passing over her face, I wasn't sure which one to follow. She leaned forward now, folding her hands in her lap.

"When you were only a few weeks old, I found her over your crib with a pillow in her hands, leaning just a couple inches over your face. I asked her what she was doing and she said she was just trying to put the pillow under your head, but that was an obvious load of crap." She went on to explain how she took Elna to see a woman who lived across the hall at the time, a retired psychologist who'd worked at an elementary school. The woman said that Elna's reaction was upsetting but within the *realm of normalcy.* A lot of toddlers had anger toward new babies. A lot of toddlers acted out. "She told me to just keep an eye on it," Candace said, shrugging. "So, I did. But then when you were about six months old, something else happened."

I found myself leaning far back from her, pressing myself into the chair and crossing my knees toward the door. My face felt hot. My palms were clammy. I wasn't really sure if I wanted to hear what else she had to say, but at the same time it felt more important than anything anyone had ever told me. Inside my mouth, I bit down on the tip of my tongue until it hurt.

"I was giving you a bath and I forgot I left the kettle on the stove. It was screaming and hissing from the kitchen and I had to shut the flame off, but you were all covered in soap. I told Elna to just watch you for a minute. Not even a minute." She glanced up at me. "Ten, fifteen seconds, maybe. I ran as fast as I could. But when I came back to the bathroom, I didn't see you. And at first, I didn't understand what was happening, but then I realized Elna had you under the water. She was just kind of looking down into the tub with her hand on your chest."

She described reaching into the bath and pulling me out. How I was quiet at first. No screaming, no sputtering. "I think that was the scariest moment of my life," she muttered, resting her hands on her knees and looking me up and down with big, wet eyes. I had no idea what to say. I thought of what happened the night before in the hotel pool and felt my pulse quicken. I began to wonder if my mother knew about it, if she tried harder to keep me in Mineral as a baby because she thought I might not survive living here. Maybe I wouldn't have, I realized. I felt a real shudder of fear then. A heave in my stomach.

Finally, Candace went on, "I have to tell you, Ida, I was so worried she'd managed to give you brain damage or something. Like, how could I know how long a baby can go without breathing? I wasn't about to take you to the hospital. They would've called social services on me in a second." She snapped her fingers in the air and raised one eyebrow, shaking her head slowly. She spoke to me like a friend, as if we were two women in a bathroom lounge sharing overdue gossip. "Oh my god, I was just so upset with Elna. And so terrified there'd be something wrong with you. But then time passed, and Anne told me you were turning out to be like, really smart, so that was a big relief."

"Everyone does think there's something wrong with me, though," I said, frowning.

"Oh well, yeah. I know that."

"How do you know?"

"I mean, it's not like my sister and I don't talk." With one hand, she pantomimed a phone held up to her ear. I noticed her movements were getting kind of slow, like she was wading through a vat of syrup. My eyes fell to the pill bottles and then back to Candace. Suddenly I felt intensely worried about what conversations the two of them might have had about me. The worry was so big, it cast a shadow over everything else Candace had just told me. The worry was familiar, too. It reminded me of how I felt in Mr. Carter's office, knowing I was the problem but never really understanding exactly why or what I could do to fix it. I went to the filing cabinet in my brain and started to sort through the years, counting backward from the present. It was full of things colored by that same kind of worry. That urgent, panicked shame I could never quite shake off. They were all in there just waiting, like clips from a movie.

Taking a spelling test in my third-grade classroom while my

teacher cut up an apple at her desk. The sound of the knife scraping against the plate. And then me, jumping out of my chair and running out into the hall. The eruption of laughter.

Being approached by the principal in the hallway for what I later learned was a high five, and just squinting at his open, outstretched palm for a long moment before tentatively pressing one finger against it, like I was pushing a button, then walking away without a word. It was the best thing I could come up with in the moment, and I could tell it wasn't exactly correct, but I didn't know what he wanted from me.

All the times I wrote in the wrong column on a quiz or up at the chalkboard because I couldn't really tell left and right apart and didn't want to admit that to anybody even though it meant getting scolded for not paying attention to instructions or purposefully ignoring them.

There were a thousand things they could've talked about on the phone. They probably talked about things I didn't even notice or know about, things that I didn't think were bad or strange but other people did. I felt so uncomfortable about it all I began to wish I could put myself, my whole body, inside the chair I was sitting in. I wanted to fold myself beneath the upholstery and stay there, silent and invisible. I wanted to never be perceived again.

"Hey," Candace said. She snapped her fingers in the air before her, trying to get my attention. I think she could tell I was feeling self-conscious. Noticing her noticing me made me even more anxious. I forced my face to relax and sat up straight again. "It's really no big deal," she said, pulling a cigarette from a box on the table and lighting it. She took a deep pull and exhaled. "Takes all kinds, right? Go on a walk for half an hour, you'll see every type of person you could imagine out there." She gestured loosely toward the window. I felt a little less bad, hearing her say that. I could tell she wasn't just telling me it because she was family, or even to try and make me feel better, but because she believed it was the truth.

A little smile came over her mouth. "You know, I used to tell Anne you reminded me of our cousin Steve. She said you reminded her of him, too."

"I've never heard about him."

"She really never mentioned Steve?"

"No. Never. I would remember."

"Huh," she said, looking into her lap with careful consideration, then back up at me. "Well, he lived nearby when we were growing up in Idaho, so he was around pretty often. He was a little older than us. Very sweet guy once you got to know him. Really bright, like you could ask him about anything and he'd have all this information just ready to go. I always thought he was hilarious. He just had the funniest observations about things. But he had a really hard time at school, just like you." She pointed at me, and some ash dropped off the tip of her cigarette and landed on her foot. She didn't seem to notice. "People were awful to him. He became incredibly shy and nervous. I was always worried he was going to like, hang himself or something, it got to be so bad."

"What happened to him?" I asked, growing worried myself.

"I haven't spoken to him in years, honestly. But I know he got some crazy job studying ancient ice."

"Like core ice?" I asked. There was an article in *Popular Science,* which we stocked at the shop, that explained how deep sections of ice could reveal things about rainfall and wind patterns and volcanic eruptions from millions of years in the past.

"I guess. Last thing I heard he was traveling to all these freezing places in the world, just yanking ice out of the ground. Oh, and he met some German woman on the job and they got married." She sat back against the couch, exhaling. "You should talk to him," she added, her face brightening up. A limp grin spread over her lips. Her eyelids were getting very droopy. "I'll track down his number for you—I know I have it somewhere." She lurched forward as if to get off the sofa and go hunting for it, but then collapsed back against the cushion. Her head slumped onto her shoulder. I watched as her cigarette slipped from her fingers and rolled onto a throw pillow. I grabbed it, wiping the ash from the fabric, and put it out.

There was a strange new feeling forming somewhere deep in my chest. I wanted to meet Steve. I wanted to see for myself why people thought we were alike. I wanted to ask him a thousand questions. Not just about the core ice, but about his life. How he made it to the other side of adolescence. If he'd had a feeling, like I did, that there was something bright waiting for him just over the horizon. And if he ever worried, the way I sometimes did, that he wouldn't have the strength to make it all the way. So many years sat in between me in this moment and the haven of my future self. I knew I'd have to be the one to get myself there. I knew that nothing was promised.

I stared at Candace's face. Her false lashes fluttered against the thin, crepey skin under her eyes. I noticed a little scar above her lip, a smattering of freckles just beneath her jawline. As I studied her, I started to think about what she'd told me, about what happened in the tub when I was a baby. I listened to the sound of the water running in the bathroom down the hall and a cold chill spread over my skin. I thought about Elna telling me the story of the two of them making it all the way up near Reno, meaning to come and get me, and then turning around. I wondered if it was because Candace couldn't handle it, or if it was because she was afraid of what Elna might do. And it hit me then, with a hard twist of dread deep in my gut, how afraid *I* was of what Elna might do.

I waited, listening again for the sound of her still preoccupied in the bathroom, then slipped quietly into the kitchen. When I switched the light on, I saw a few fat, shiny cockroaches scurrying back behind the stove. I shivered. There was a little window above the sink left open a crack. Some pink, glass-angel figurines sat on the ledge, all in different positions of prayer. Even with the cool air blowing in, I could smell something sour and rancid coming from the fridge.

I took the phone off the hook and leaned back against the opposite counter, trying to breathe through my mouth. I held the receiver in my hand for a moment, just staring at it, before deciding to punch in Jen's number. I couldn't bear the thought of hearing my mother's voice, just the idea of it made my face sear with guilt and anger, but I knew I couldn't stay here in this apartment much longer. I knew Jen would be checking her messages at home, and I knew she understood me well enough to wonder if I wouldn't be more likely to call her before I called the store. It rang five times, then I heard her voice on the recording.

You've got Jen, she grunted. *Leave a message.*

"It's me," I whispered. I paused for a moment, unsure of what to say next. "I really messed up." I tugged at the hem of my shirt. There were some loose pieces of bread crust on the ground, blue with mold. I kicked them under the cabinet. "I know it was stupid of me to run away. I'm in San Francisco." The refrigerator made a weak humming sound, like it was trying to will itself to work, before sputtering out. "I need you to come get me." Tears sprung fast into my eyes when I said that. I cupped my hand over my mouth and bent my head down for a moment, trying to steady the feeling that was roiling up in me. I wiped the tears with my sleeve and took a deep breath. I bit my lip to try and keep it all in. Then I straightened up and said simply, "Bye," before putting the phone back on the hook.

Another cockroach emerged from beneath the sink. I watched its long antennae quivering in the breeze. I'd seen a twenty-four-hour diner nearby when we were driving in, and I wondered whether I should try to slip out quietly and just sit there, waiting. I knew it would be a while before Jen could get to me, but the idea of staying in the apartment any longer made my stomach turn. So too, though, did the idea of wandering around a web of noisy, unfamiliar streets, trying to find a place I'd glimpsed only in passing, and didn't even know the name of. Besides, I reasoned, I couldn't go someplace where Jen wouldn't know to look for me.

At that moment, a tingling sensation passed over my skin, and when I turned around, Elna was standing there in the doorway in a green bathrobe, her wet hair hanging all around her shoulders.

"What are you doing?" she asked.

"Nothing," I said.

"I heard you talking to someone. Who were you on the phone with?"

"Just the pharmacy," I blurted out, relieved and a little surprised at my quick thinking.

"Why?"

"She asked me to call and see if she had any refills waiting," I said, pointing toward Candace out on the sofa.

"And you did it?"

"Well, I—"

"When she asks you to do things like that," Elna cut me off, "don't."

"Okay."

Elna turned around and stared into the living room, then looked back at me. "How many did she take while I was in the shower?"

"I don't know, a few."

"She'll be out for a couple hours, probably." Elna sighed.

"Should we try to move her to her bed, or something?"

"No," she said. "It doesn't matter."

"All right."

"You two have a good chat?" she asked, reaching to take me by the hand and leading me out of the kitchen back toward the sofa. She scrunched at her hair, casting an annoyed look down onto Candace, whose eyes were fluttering. I could see flashes of the whites between her lashes. The corner of her mouth drooped. I felt like I should cover her with a blanket.

Before I could answer Elna's question, she said, "Oh, wait a second," then walked over to a shelf by the sofa. She looked through the mess of books and papers, then pulled out a small photo album. It was white leather with a gold-embossed trim. She flipped through the laminated pages before stopping on one in the middle. There was Candace, lying back in a hospital bed. She wore a blue cotton robe with the top pulled open, chest exposed. A naked baby with wrinkly, purple-looking skin lay face down against her breast, legs curled up. Me, I understood. There was my bean-shaped birthmark, just in between the shoulders. A little orange date code in the corner read, *Feb-1-83.*

"Just in case you still thought I was bullshitting you," Elna said. She slammed the album shut and dropped it on the coffee table, sending the pill bottles rolling to the floor. "Come on," she said. "Let's go to my room for a bit."

26

Her room was very small. Not much bigger than the storage closet at the shop. And there were piles of clothes everywhere. Skirts and dresses and expensive-looking sweaters draped all around. They all had their tags dangling from the sides. Some even had security clamps still stuck in the fabric. In the corner by the window, I noticed a big Tupperware container on top of a towel, full of these clamps. They were burnt and warped, melted with blackened coils popping out from the middles. Next to the container was a lighter and a pair of pliers. The smell of hot plastic lingered faintly in the air. She took her robe off and got dressed half standing in the closet, pulling some clothes out from one of the many piles and covering her wet hair with a fuzzy purple bucket hat.

Before this moment, I'd imagined Elna's room like one of the pictures from the magazine spreads I spent so much time studying. Clean and bright, with a canopy bed and a telephone. And I felt angry at myself then, actually being there and seeing how different it was from those pictures. Of course it wasn't like a magazine. I should've known better than to think it could've been. She did have a white vanity table with a light-up mirror, but there was a crack in the glass and the countertop was piled high with unopened cosmetics. Three or four of the same eye shadow palette stacked together. Six bottles of the same perfume in a row. I caught a glimpse of my face in the mirror and jumped a little bit, startled. For a flash of a moment, I thought I was somebody else. Slowly, I raised my hand up, keeping my eyes on the reflection. Nothing about my face felt familiar. I turned away then, unsettled.

I asked Elna, "Why do you have all this stuff?"

"To sell," she said. "But I have to get rid of it all before I go to LA. I don't want to bring a ton of junk down there." The things on the vanity, she explained, came from a friend who worked in the stockroom at a beauty supply store. Every week, they'd load the friend's car full of the stash from Elna's room and go around to different places, selling from the trunk. "Do you want any of it?" she asked. I shook my head no. "Then let's go up to the roof for a while," she said. "I can't stand to be in this apartment right now. It smells like rotten chicken."

We walked past Candace, still asleep on the couch surrounded by pillows and candles and the smog of incense, out into the building's hallway, where we went through a rusty old door and climbed seven floors up, emerging through another rusty old door into the night air. There were some plastic lawn chairs sitting around, a couple of them tipped onto their sides, and a big puddle of rainwater in the center of them, where the roof seemed to sink in. The climb had made my heart twinge a little and I stopped, instinctively pressing my hand against my chest to feel for my pulse. It stuttered for a moment, trying to find its rhythm, before slowly coming back. I took deep breaths, drawing the cold breeze into my lungs and then letting it out, trying to steady myself.

"You all right?" Elna asked.

"Fine," I said.

Out on the distant horizon, I could see a shining, black slick of water. Ship lights moved over the surface. There was the bridge again, twinkling above the bay. I walked over near the roof's edge and looked out, pulling my coat tight around me. Wisps of fog hung around the bridge's cables. From where I stood, they all seemed so small. Little golden threads against a dark sky. I took another step and peeked over the side. Seven stories down, two people meandered through the street with a rickety shopping cart. I could hear the screech of its wheels all the way up here. There was a laundromat with a blinking neon sign. A boarded-up shop next door with a poster that read, *Shoes fixed in ten minutes.*

When I turned around, I saw Elna nudging a floor tile with her toe. She wiggled it around, wedged it loose at the edge, and then crouched down to dig beneath it with her fingers. She pulled out a plastic bag and unfurled it, holding it up to the floodlight and giving it a careful look.

"Have you ever gotten high before?" she asked. I told her no. "First time for everything," she said. "I bet you could really use it after the last few days." A dry laugh escaped her mouth, but she wasn't smiling. We sat together on the lawn chairs, facing out toward the bridge. I watched her take another plastic bag out from the first one. A sweet, skunky smell floated out from inside. "It's just weed," she said. "Nothing crazy." She held a chunk of it in one hand and broke off little bits with her fingers, crushing them up and then sprinkling them into a purple glass pipe.

"Why do you keep it up here in the floor?" I asked.

"Candace." She sighed.

"She'd be mad?"

"What? No. She'd take it and smoke it all herself." Elna pulled a lighter from her pocket and used the bottom end to press the weed down flat in the pipe. Then she lit it, moving the flame around in a circle, tapping her thumb over a little hole in the side of the glass as she drew smoke into her mouth. She held it for a while, only exhaling when her face turned red.

"Here," she said, leaning over toward me. "Let me show you." Some of her wet hair had fallen loose from under her hat. It brushed against my cheek as she moved. I thought of the way it looked in the motel pool, beads of water rolling off it, how it clung to her skin. I could smell chlorine, just faintly, when I pictured it. Another piece fell against my face as she wriggled her chair nearer.

"No," I said, jerking back. "I get how to do it." She stopped, staring at me.

"Okay," she said. The word came out slow, a little hesitant. Her eyes followed as I took the pipe and copied everything she'd done. I wasn't so sure that I wanted to be doing it at all, not like this. It wasn't that I never got curious about getting high. Last summer, I'd kept an eye out at the lake for ends of discarded joints by the firepit, thinking maybe I could try a little that way. Like most things, it seemed like an activity better done alone. After what happened with the diving board, though, it just seemed easier not to say no to Elna.

At first, I felt nothing but a tingling in my lungs and a burning, sour feeling in my throat. I blew the smoke back out and waited a few minutes, coughing, then brought the pipe back to my lips and inhaled again, reigniting the little embers as I pulled more air. I held it until my eyes watered.

Elna smiled at me, one brow arched in amused surprise. "Look at you," she said, chuckling.

I touched my hair, thinking there must be something stuck in it. It felt incredibly soft. I ran my fingers through it again and again, reveling in the texture.

"I didn't know if you'd like it or not," she said. "I wasn't sure if you'd even try it."

"I do like it." I reached for the pipe again, taking another big gulp of smoke. It felt like a balloon had begun to inflate somewhere in my gut and was rising slowly, gently into my brain.

"Watch it," Elna said, still giggling. "You're taking really big hits."

"It's fine," I told her.

"Do you feel it yet?" she asked.

"Yeah," I said. Then, a few moments later, "I think this is the first time I've ever actually felt relaxed." At this, she burst into laughter. “I’m not kidding,” I added. “I think it really is.” It was different than how I felt looking at maps or diving. Lighter. Easier. Like my body was suddenly something I could sit comfortably inside of instead of trying to escape. Elna took the pipe from me and had some more. Smoke puffed from her nostrils. She set everything down in her lap, her face suddenly serious.

“Well?” she asked. “Are you happy?”

“What do you mean?”

“You’re home, kind of,” she replied.

“Home,” I repeated.

“I mean, I took you out of that crappy little town and brought you back. Everyone else was too scared to do that.”

She crumbled some more into the bowl and pressed it down again, taking a quick inhale before passing it back to me. This time, I held it in my lungs until I felt like I was going to faint. My pulse skipped around a little. I moved to put my fingers to my chest out of habit, then stopped midair. I waited. I felt the muscle of my heart flutter and twitch. After a minute, it leveled out and I let my hand fall to the side. Elna didn’t seem to notice. She was peeling polish off her fingernails.

“Wouldn’t you rather be here with me?” she asked. “Like, if your other option is selling Hostess cakes to perverts all day?” I nodded, because it seemed like the correct reaction. Really, I would have rather been in a cave on an uncharted island. I would have rather been on the surface of the moon. “So,” she went on, her voice hoarse, “welcome home, weirdo.”

“Thank you,” I choked out. “But I don’t really feel at home.”

"You'll get used to San Francisco soon."

"No, like, I don't feel at home in the world."

Elna looked at me with a pinched-up expression, her mouth twisted into a pursed little frown and eyes wide. "God, that's so depressing, Ida," she finally said. I stared at her. A foghorn sounded somewhere off in the distance on the water.

"Oh, sorry," I replied. "It doesn't have to be depressing. I just meant it as like, a statement of fact." My lips began to feel like they were falling off my face. I reached my hand up and patted them carefully. Elna burst out laughing. She leaned forward, her hair spilling down in front, as she shook and gasped for air. Her hat fell off her head and plopped into the puddle of rainwater. She left it sitting there.

"Oh my god," she said. "You are so funny sometimes. Do you know that? I don't think you really know that." She wiped a tear from her left eye.

I didn't care if she thought I was funny. I didn't even care anymore if she liked me. I tilted my head back and looked up at the sky. Almost all the stars were covered by fog and city lights. Only a few twinkling specks. In Mineral, I could count hundreds of them. I saw comets from the backyard. I'd seen a meteor shower. I loved to lie in the grass, just watching, and think about many millions of years in the future when humans were long gone from the Earth, and how even then, every night, blazing orange stars would streak through the dark, leaving long trails of sparkling dust in their wake. I liked that these spectacular displays were completely indifferent to my gaze.

"What are you thinking about?" Elna asked.

"I'm wondering why my mouth is so dry," I told her, still looking at the sky.

"That's just what happens. People call it cottonmouth."

"Feels weird." I swallowed, and noticed the sides of my throat sticking together.

"So." She crossed her legs and leaned back in her lawn chair. "What did you two talk about while I was washing my hair?"

"Politics," I said.

"What?" she said. She swiveled her head around and squinted at me. "Is this you joking on purpose?"

"We talked about what you told me, Elna."

"Yeah, of course, but what did she say?"

"I don't know," I muttered.

"You were alone for a while. Must have been something."

"Just like, that it was hard having a baby."

"Right." She twirled the lighter around between her fingers, scoffing. Then she started tossing it up in the air and catching it, grabbing it harder each time. "You know," she said. "I don't know if I've ever seen her smile the way she smiled at you when we came in tonight."

"I'm sure you have," I replied. I didn't know why I said that. I had no idea what kinds of smiles Elna had seen on Candace or anyone else.

"No," she insisted. "I really haven't."

"Well, it's been almost five years."

"I know how long it's been," Elna said. She looked at me

straight-on, unblinking. I turned away but I could still sense her eyes on me. A prickling sensation spread over my skin.

I got up and walked over to the corner of the roof. I needed space. I took deep breaths, trying to tamp down my growing overwhelm. Visions of Candace's loose, toothy grin looped in my mind, swirling with Elna's hardened stare. Suddenly, everything felt awful. My hands were like big, cartoon gloves that couldn't be taken off. My heart raced. All I wanted to do was be still and quiet in the cool air, looking at the bridge out on the water. It appeared so much brighter now. Glowing. A bridge made of smoldering, gilt embers. Headlights blurred all along it.

I couldn't tell if a few seconds had passed or if I'd been standing over there for a long time. Thinking about it made me anxious. I didn't know what to do anymore. The whole way on the road, even when I felt miserable, there was at least some purpose to it. I knew what I was waiting on. I knew why I was there. Now, I realized I had no idea what would happen next. I didn't even know where I would sleep that night. The idea of sleeping next to Elna made my heart race even harder. I couldn't stomach it. I felt a surge of anger rolling up in me like a wave. It wasn't toward myself this time, though. It was at her.

I heard footsteps behind me and turned around. There was Elna, standing just a few feet away. She'd taken her jacket off and left it on the ground. Now she was only wearing a T-shirt. Her arms were pale and bony. Her face was scrubbed clean from the shower. There were dark circles under her eyes. We stood there, just staring at each other. The air around us seemed to pulse. I found myself thinking about the feeling of her hand on top of my head in the pool. And about how now, no matter what, after that and after what had happened at the lake, diving could never mean the same thing to me again. It was the one thing I'd found that let me be really, truly alone in the way I so desperately needed. It belonged to me so completely. It made my life bearable. And one day, Elna walked through the front door of the shop and quickly ruined it. I thought too about how small I must have been when she'd held me under in the tub, years ago. My whole hand couldn't have been much bigger than a walnut. Something about that got to me. The smallness.

I didn't push it all down this time like the other night at the motel. The wave of anger, the fast crush of thoughts. I couldn't have, even if I wanted to. There was nowhere for my thoughts to escape to. Every sound from the city below seemed to be amplified. Every light left smeary, glowing trails in my vision as I moved my eyes. My heart was really racing now. I noticed the beats were getting uneven. Skipping three, four in a row and then desperately pushing to make up for it, pounding away. Black dots started to appear at the edges of my vision.

"We were in the middle of a conversation," Elna said. "Don't you know it's rude to just get up and walk away?" A mean smirk settled on her lips.

"Let's keep having it, then," I replied. I tried to muster what I thought was a sarcastic smile through the dizziness and the searing anger. Elna stared at me expectantly, one hand on her hip. Nearly every bit of polish had chipped off her nails. As I looked at them, echoes of their grip on my scalp rippled over my skin. I thought back to weeks earlier at the store, those fingers smudging blush into my cheeks, her saying I was like her own little doll. The way happy butterflies shot through my stomach when she said it.

Now, on the roof, it felt like I was just suddenly getting the joke. Getting that there *was* a joke, and that it was on me. Elna had been playing with me since she first walked through the door of the shop in a burst of cold air. Making me up in mascara and glitter, making me think we were friends, then ruining it all just to build it up again for fun. She wanted to see how far I would go, how much I would tolerate. She dragged me around, all the way to this far-off city, and I just went along. Limp, accepting, like I had buttons for eyes. Now I wanted her to let me go.

Gathering all the strength in my body, I looked at her straight-on and said, "Candace told me she always wished she'd sent you away, instead. That she kept the wrong daughter." Elna was still for a moment. It was almost as if she hadn't heard me.

She started to walk away, back toward the door to the stairwell, but then stopped, standing still for another moment. Suddenly, she turned on her heel and broke into a run toward me. This felt different than with Tom, whose movement across the ice came in fast blurs, like a spider crawling across the floor. Elna appeared to move in slow motion. Her hair whipped around her face, her green eyes flashed under the glare of the floodlight. Her T-shirt hem, flapping in the wind. Two rows of gleaming white teeth. I tried to steady myself against my fluttering heart. More black spots came into my vision. She reached her hands out toward me. I could see the lines in her palms. I could see the blue veins in her wrists. There came a searingly sharp pain in my chest, the worst I'd ever felt in my life. I could sense my brain losing contact with my body, my knees starting to buckle as I wobbled to the side, unable to find my balance.

And then, nothing.

27

I woke up near the edge of the roof with a dull, throbbing pain at the back of my head. I sat up slowly, reaching around and feeling something wet in my hair. For a while, I just stayed in place, staring down at my hand. There was blood on my fingertips. Ringing in my ears.

I stood up and looked around. The roof was empty. There was the cluster of lawn chairs in the middle, the plastic bag of weed left on one of them, still open. The dingy pool of trapped rainwater. The floodlight above the door. And there was Elna's hat and coat, lying on the tiles. It had begun to rain a little bit. A gentle sprinkling coming down from the fog layer. I didn't see Elna anywhere. I looked around the other side of the roof, where there was a small grill tipped over on its side and a broken umbrella. I even checked in the stairwell, popping my head inside and calling out her name. My own voice echoed back to me.

And then I looked over the edge.

There was Elna, splayed out on the sidewalk below. Her arms and legs were twisted at strange angles. One wrist bent completely the wrong way. But her face was serene. It almost looked like she was sleeping, but for the dark puddle of blood blooming around her head like a halo. I don't know how long I stood there, staring down. The blood puddle spilled over the curb and formed a river down into a sewer grate. I remember someone standing over her, their hands clapped over their mouth, then three others rushing up to her body. The sound of a woman letting out a short scream. Then there was a siren. It started low in the distance and grew louder, shrieking as it arrived on the block. Blue, red flashing lights. A few men in dark uniforms running with a stretcher. She was limp when they lifted her, hair dragging along the ground. One of them looked up at me.

EPILOGUE

I spent that whole night in the hospital getting stitches on the back of my head and giving my statement to the police. Candace took me to the bathroom, alone, before they arrived at my bedside. She turned the faucet on and said, very quietly, right into my ear, "If you ever listen to me about anything in your life, let it be this. You tell them Elna was suicidal after my relapsing again, and when you tried to stop her from going over the edge, she shoved you to the ground and jumped anyway." I listened.

Very early in the morning, Jen arrived in San Francisco to take me home. It turned out she'd been driving only a few hours behind us, leaving on Christmas Day after being shown the note I'd left and suspecting where we were headed. Anne stayed at the store by the phone, just in case. The way back felt three times as long as the trip down. We didn't talk much, but we did stop at a motel to rest and call Mineral. There was a carnival in a field across the way, and Jen took me up for a long ride on the Ferris wheel.

"Things are going to be better now," she said. Candace was sent back to state rehab and put on parole for violating the terms of her early release. Some months later, her number was disconnected, and mail came back marked *Return to sender.* On my eighteenth birthday, I got a postcard from Acapulco with a messy lipstick kiss right on the back and one written line: *To my baby girl.* After that, I never heard from Candace again.

Patrick's car was returned to him, undamaged, at our expense. I wrote him a note, apologizing for the theft, which I left in the Arthurs' mailbox. A few days later, he approached me in the yard to say that he wasn't "sour" over it. He asked me if I'd actually driven it myself and I told him no, I hadn't. Soon, he was teaching me to parallel-park out on the street. I let him know how much I loved *Jar of Flies* and, thrilled, he introduced me to what would become all my other favorite albums.

I never said anything about Tom, to anyone. The sheriff came to our place twice, first to ask my mother about her observations of him as a tenant, and then to search his room for anything that might explain his disappearance. Some drugs and cash and stolen materials from the new logging site were found under his futon. In spring, when the ice melted, his bloated remains washed ashore, and his death was deemed accidental.

I never went back to school, either. Once my head wound healed, I gave a lengthy presentation in the kitchen on why I should be allowed to homeschool myself. No one argued. So, I did. Every day for the next three years at the desk in my room.

My mother signed off on my mandated standardized tests and sealed them in a State Department of Education envelope, which I walked over to the post office once a quarter. I went on to the University of Washington and got a degree in physical geography, double-majoring in geomorphology and oceanography, before finding a job with the National Ocean Service's newly established Coral Reef Conservation Program. My first surveying assignment was in Palau.

In 2012, I returned to Mineral to attend Jen and my mother's wedding. By then, I'd just started seeing the person I would eventually go on to marry myself: Kate, a professor of marine hydrology I met while working in Guam. I woke up early in my old bedroom the morning of my mother and Jen's ceremony and hiked the trail up to Needle Lake, alone, under the canopy of the same ancient trees I'd known as a teenager. When I got to the top, I stood on the edge of the dock for a long time, looking out at the sun rising over the pines. And then, I dove in.

ACKNOWLEDGMENTS

With deepest gratitude to:

Samantha, Katy, Whitney, Debbie, Rachel, Corina, Aarushi, Samara, Kira, Margueya, Molly, Laura, Channa, Isabel, Mary, Audrey, Lauren, Kasi, Natalie.

ABOUT THE AUTHOR

JUSTINE CHAMPINE's short fiction has appeared in *The Kenyon Review*, *Epoch*, and the *Los Angeles Review of Books*. She holds an MFA from Sarah Lawrence College and lives in New York City. *Needle Lake* is her second novel, after her debut, *Knife River*.

justinechampine.com
Instagram: @justine_champine

Books Driven by the Heart

Sign up for our newsletter and find more you'll love:

thedialpress.com

@THEDIALPRESS

@THEDIALPRESS